Danny Dowling is a man from Exeter, Devon, with a massive imagination. Danny has filled various roles in life; former professional athlete in Taekwondo, amateur stage actor, fitness instructor and now writer and creator. Danny has always been fascinated and captivated by the incredible worlds created by artists throughout history and is excited to hopefully capture the imagination of every reader of his work.

Thank you to everyone that encouraged me to show this to the world.

Thank you to my family and my friends for your support.

Moreover, I would like to thank Adam Brown for his amazing artwork for the cover and Jonny Leach for creating the title logo.

Danny Dowling

TALES OF THE TURNIP KNIGHT

AUSTIN MACAULEY PUBLISHERS™

LONDON • CAMBRIDGE • NEW YORK • SHARJAH

A CIP catalogue record for this title is available from the British Library.

ISBN 9781398429529 (Paperback)
ISBN 9781398429543 (ePub-e-book)
ISBN 9781398429536 (Adiobook)

www.austinmacauley.com

First Published 2022
Austin Macauley Publishers Ltd®
1 Canada Square
Canary Wharf
London
E14 5AA

"There is a prophecy…

"When the world is on its last legs, when evil, hate, tyranny and oppression have dominated over all else and there is no hope left for justice and truth, there will be a dark figure arising from the horizon.

"It is said he has the power of a thousand mages in each of his fingernails and a sword so sharp that the he can cut away the air itself and leave his enemies without anything to breathe. He will walk vast and distant lands, freeing the innocent and stamping out injustice and tyranny with a stare so intense, and with such resolve that a man with an impure heart would die at a glance.

"And the name of this man, I hear you ask? He is known only as the Turnip Knight."

"A hero is not measured by the strength of his sword, but by the strength of his justice."

I

The sun rose over Dragon's Peak and began to pierce in through the windows of the wood huts of Doko Village. Soon the men will stir and prepare for another day of labour; tending to crops, catching the fish of the lake to the south, along with the other day-to-day chores. But one boy is already awake, standing tall atop his home in the South Westerly area of the village. With the morning breeze blowing in his rough cut blonde hair, poking through the holes of his hollowed wooden helmet, Derek, the self-proclaimed Turnip Knight in training, took in the scene that is his home before his morning training.

With a twist and a flip (it was in fact a small hop), he placed his foot onto the crates that stack like stairs next to his home and descended to the next three lower crates before majestically leaping the two-foot drop to the ground (he'd jump from the top but his mum says he'll hurt himself; he is a warrior in training after all). Derek set off at a brisk pace to the East, towards Bikhin Forest. With the morning sun in his eyes, he dodged and dived (even throwing in the occasional rolly poly) to avoid being blinded by the sharp sunlight. Derek had learnt to always be on his guard, even in his peaceful village, and didn't want the sun to be blinding him should he need to engage in a battle.

Before too long, Derek reached Bikhin Forest and began the natural assault course that he had done every day for nearly a year. It had been almost a year to the day since he was told the story of the Turnip Knight by his mother before bed time. Being eight years old now, he felt stronger than ever and ready to reach the next level on his way to achieving the rank of the Ultimate Turnip Knight. Some of the other locals have tried to reason with him and tell him that Turnip Knights don't exist and that he should think about joining the Royal Guards in the major city Zeehan and perhaps, if he works really hard, he could become a Zeehan Sir (but more on them later, let's concentrate on Derek for now). But Derek is sure of himself and believes that once he becomes a Turnip Knight for real, even the Zeehan Sirs would consider him their superior.

He jumped left and right on the exposed roots of the ancient trees as he made his way deeper in. Swinging from vine to vine, he then began ascending the bridge tree. The bridge tree hangs over the edge of a massive drop into a deep ravine but happens to extend far enough that you can, in theory, climb across it and jump down on the other side of the waterfall without using the safe rope bridge. Derek could see the long, wide branches that extend the full way across the ravine. His eyes narrowed as he considered his route, and he carefully descended the tree and walked across the safe rope bridge towards his practice tree.

Derek reached the practice tree, and with the piercing blades of sunlight through the gaps in the leaves above, Derek unsheathed his wooden justice sword from his make shift holster (a shred of old rabbit skin that he's tied around his leather belt that he got last Christmas), and began to engage in almighty battle with his worthy sparring partner, the tree. For hours, Derek ducked, dodged and dived while also furiously whipping and slashing his mighty wooden justice sword, occasionally launching a flying foot frenzy and back elbow at the familiar advisory. Bits and bulks of bark burst away from the practice tree showering the surrounding forest floor. If an enemy could see him now, they'd run away for sure.

"I'm getting hungry," he told himself as he bowed respectfully to the tree that had impressively withstood his arsenal of assault for another day.

"See ya tomorrow practice tree." With his wooden justice sword safely back at his hip, Derek waved his practice tree goodbye as he jogged back towards the safe rope bridge on his way to a nice helping of his mother's stew left over from last night.

II

It was another fine morning in Doko Village. Deegal Dimmie, a diamond and rare gemstone forager, and Rhadia Flohgan, a lumberjack, were both up and about starting their stoves and stretching their muscles, enjoying the sun-shine as it shone on their tranquil land. The smell of meat and simmering vegetables began to fill the air, marking another start to another day of labour and hard graft.

Derek jogged back home, weaving in and out around the other huts excitedly while thinking about the food that will greet him when he returned safely home after a morning of hard training. He exchanged pleasantries with the other villagers as he passed them by, sneaking peaks at their to-be breakfasts and occasionally getting the odd scrap of food passed his way.

'Well what should I expect,' Derek thought to himself. 'I am their protector in training after all.'

Grinning from ear to ear, Derek finally made it back to his home.

"Mum!" he yelled. "Hey, is breakfast ready? I'm starving!"

As Derek approached the front door to the home he'd known all eight years of his life, the face of his beloved mum poked out through the open doorway. Before Derek could even react (he had been training really hard and was pretty tired out) the thwart of an iron ladle pounded into his skull courtesy of his lovely mother.

"Derek! You didn't get the firewood like I asked you too! Were you off playing by that bloody tree *again*? That forest is dangerous, I told you not to go there." Derek reeled and writhed in pain clutching at his head and checking for blood. After rolling around on the floor for a few moments he wiped most of the tears from his eyes and stood back up.

"I'm sorry, Mum; I'll go get some wood after breakfast I promise."

"No Derek, you need to go and get the wood now, without any wood I can't make any breakfast!"

By the time Derek had gotten the fire wood and his mum had made his breakfast he was hungry enough to eat a Fleckered Nergal (Fleckered Nergals are known for their immense size, particularly around the waistline). Derek sat down on the soft mud outside his front door and began scoffing away at last night's stew that was now making, much to Derek's delight, a very good breakfast.

III

The late morning and early afternoon of the average day for the average boy (even a Turnip Knight in training, Derek's mother assures him) in Doko Village is spent learning about how to read and write, how to be a polite and respectful person, and what's what in the land. Derek has been learning now at the Doko Village learning hut for three years and, although not great at writing himself, has been able to pick up the art of reading. He's even been able to understand old scriptures from an earlier form of his language fairly well.

"So what do you think you'll be learning today, Delly?" Derek's mum asks, using the pet name he so despises.

"Muuuum, my name is Derek, not Delly."

"You're my son I'll call you what I like, have a good day today, okay? And for god sake, take that bloody wooden hat off!"

With his armour and weapons shut away in his home, Derek set off for his daily classes. Doko Village was very lucky to have an educator and he should take full advantage of that, or so his mum says. On his way to the learning hut, to the north of the village, Derek spies the bobbing of sun coloured hair (the only other blonde person in the village) to his left on the other side of a hut, heading the same direction.

13

"Ayyyye, Pip! Aye!"

Pippie Lip, Derek's class mate and friend, twisted and turned straining to find the origin of the call out. Eventually, after Derek stopped walking and stood very still, Pippie noticed the floundering waving of the arms of his friend. Unfortunately for Pippie, he noticed Derek before he noticed the iron hammer head sticking out from the abandoned tool sitting on a table, nearly knocking himself clean out with an almighty crack to the eye socket.

Derek and Pippie walked the rest of the way to the learning hut together. Pippie's dad worked in the Zeehan Kingdom, providing news to the public and Pippie wanted to follow in his footsteps and do the same when he grows up, even though the village educator, Vlan Maggie, insists that Pippie could go a lot further.

"Did you hear about Dragon's Peak?" Pippie asked his adventurous friend.

"No, what's happened?"

"Someone was up there last week; they found actual signs of a real dragon living there."

"But I thought there always were dragons living on Dragon's Peak."

"No, it's just a name, maybe it was named because there *used* to be a dragon there."

"Well maybe they didn't look hard enough."

"But that's the thing; my dad says if there were dragons living up there someone would have spotted them by now. Rare breeds are native to this country so we have a lot of Dragon Watchers that come here looking for them. But no one has seen any wild dragons in this country for years."

"So what are they going to do now then?"

"I don't know. The Zeehan committee will have to find out what breed it is and then if it's deemed too dangerous a Zeehan Sir will have to come and deal with it."

"… Hmm."

"Pretty cool though, right? Could be a Zok Dragon; fastest known flying dragon. Would explain why no one has seen it."

"Or it could be some completely new dragon, maybe one that's invisible or something! Man that'd be cool."

"… Don't be ridiculous Derek."

IV

The sun set on Doko Village with the red of the sky bleaching the overhead burgundy. Derek said goodbye to his friend Pippie after their extra time spent at the learning hut. Pippie wanted help with some of his Scriptures homework and Derek always gets help from Pippie with geography and classes regarding everything from Kingdom politics to agriculture. Derek wants to know as much as he can about the world so he can be the best Turnip Knight he can.

Home to a chimney puffing out the sweet scent of boiled vegetables and smoked meat, Derek excitedly greeted his mum and distracted his aching belly with stories of the day's events before dinner.

"Oh, Derek, there's a royal march happening in Zeehan on the weekend. Apparently Sir Neek is returning from a three-year quest from all the way in Daburan and the King is personally welcoming him back."

"Daburan? That's really far away; they even have a different language over there." Derek had just learnt about the country today.

"Yes Derek, it's a long way away and Sir Neek is a much respected knight. Seeing as you want to be a knight so badly, why don't we go? I may even treat you to a special something while we're there."

"Okay, it'll be good! I hope missing my daily training won't set me back too much."

"It's one day; you can take a break for one day."

Derek thought about the knights of the Zeehan capital as he tucked into his tea. Sir Neek is well known around the country for his strength, and many of the Zeehan Sir's are revered even further afield in neighbouring countries for their power, knowledge and skill. But one thing Zeehan didn't have was a Turnip Knight. As far as Derek knew, none of the Zeehan Sir's could even use Greater Magic, the second level of spell strength for a spellcaster. Derek wanted to be stronger with a sword than even Sir Neek, and yet be as skilled as a master level mage at spell casting, just like a Turnip Knight.

V

The weekend came about and before he knew it, Derek was on a Knark Coach; a people carrying cart powered by a tamed Knark (Knarks are Hippo sized, purple, one-eyed creatures that live on a diet of stinging nettles and earth worms) and on his way to the grand capital city of Zeehan.

Derek held his mum's hand so as not to get lost or snatched by one of the evil syndicates that you'd expect of a major city, and as he breached the grand entrance to the capital, his eyes widened and bulged as he took in the vast size of the place. Being a boy of a village, Derek rarely went to the major city as it was mainly occupied by businessmen, adventurer guilds, thieves and the military. There were of course merchants, but their general way of making a living had to be the same as cut-throat businessmen if they wanted to stay afloat. Seeing as Derek was an eight-year-old boy with no business experience or willingness to pickpocket unsuspecting passers-by, Derek didn't really feel like he needed to go to the big city all that often. 'When I'm a super strong Turnip Knight, I'll come and get famous in the city, until then, I'll just train hard out of sight in the country,' he thought to himself.

Adventurer's Guilds, where warriors and spell casters go to take quests and earn a living, popped up occasionally amongst the different shops and pubs in the streets. Weapon shops, armour shops and magic shops were also not in short supply. Derek was on the brink of breaking his neck as he struggled to scout them all from the safety of his mum's grip.

"Zeehan is known as the Adventurers Country, Derek. We have a long history of producing some of the best adventurers, some of the best even go on to join the Zeehan guards and even become Zeehan Sirs."

"Adventurers?"

"They travel the land, getting into all sorts of trouble, living by their wits and instinct. Sometimes they create alliances to get harder jobs done, and build friendships."

"Is that where Dad is now? Off on an adventure with friends?"

"He might be, but knowing your father, he's probably taking on more than he should by himself!"

After a few minutes, they reached the Grand Walk; a decorative sapphire and gold coloured road that leads from the city centre markets to the royal palace. They had gotten there extremely early so they could get a place right at the front. Soon, more people began to gather and chatter amongst the crowd grew louder as everyone anticipated the return of the decorated Sir Neek. Townsman speculated on the kind of task he was put on that required him to travel so far and for so long. Others spouted the rumours that he wasn't successful in his task, or that he was nearly fatally injured, and even that his task was not set by the King but he went anyway. Derek's imagination ran wild, thinking of all the possible things that happened during Sir Neek's quest, and began to really anticipate seeing him.

VI

An hour passed and the Grand Walk was now swamped with townspeople that came to see Sir Neek. A small number of royal guards lined the pathway to deter criminals or people running on to the walkway. Before too long, trumpets roared in unison and a large entourage of knights walked towards the great castle. The screams of the onlookers were deafening as the armour clad group drew nearer to where Derek was standing. Eight well-dressed knights, who were in the army as knights more for their charisma and looks than fighting skill, walked with a lone figure in the middle.

Sir Neek's armour was beaten and dented to near scrap. The Zeehan crest that glistened in the sunlight of the other knight's armour was all but completely ripped from his chest. His face was cut and bruised and he looked to Derek like he was so worn out that the walk itself was a challenge. The near oblivious crowed cheered and screamed as they got taken in by Sir Neek's brave face and the work of the other eight show-off knights. The eight knights waved to the crowd and occasionally exchanged greetings with a few people, but Derek wasn't taken in by the show they were putting on.

Before long, the nine knights were closing in on the end of the Grand Walk, and to where Derek was standing. They stopped in line of Derek and the King came down to greet them. His long magisterial robe dragged along the stone of the steps as he descended from the palace. Sir Neek stood as tall as his body would allow, to greet the King. A single hand from his majesty in the air silenced the audience in an instant.

"Today we see the return of one of the most prestigious gentlemen in the whole kingdom. On his journey he faced real hardship and trial. However, Sir Burten Neek is a resilient individual and won the battles that faced him…"

Sir Neek dropped his head and a disappointed expression took over his face.

"… Today, the Kingdom of Zeehan welcomes you home, Sir Neek."

The crowd roared yet more loudly than before as everyone cheered for their returned hero. The eight other knights began to wave and appeal to the crowd once again. Derek's eyes locked with one of the knights, and he approached Derek.

The knight's brown, smartly cut hair wasn't a strand out of place, his armour was polished to a gleam and his teeth were whiter than a new stick of chalk.

"Hello there son, I'm Sir Wilzer, what's your name?" He spoke softly, as he knelt down to Derek's eye level.

"Derek."

"Little Derek, huh? Well Derek, what does your dad do? Is he a knight here?"

"No, he's an adventurer."

"Oh, an adventurer, wow. That's quite splendid, young man. And I bet you want to be an adventurer too?"

"Nope."

"No? Oh, well then what do you want to be when you grow up little Derek?"

"I want to be a Turnip Knight."

Sir Wilzer looked at Derek, puzzled for a moment, then began to smirk.

"A Turnip Knight? But that's just a story, little Derek, I don't think you could be one of those."

"No! I'm going to be a Turnip Knight!"

Sir Neek, who up to this point had completely ignored the entire crowd, turned towards Derek, his face a ghostly white and his eyes widened as he turned himself face to face with Derek.

Derek's and Neek's eyes met, drawing the attention of Wilzer, Derek's mum, and even some of the onlookers. Neek continued a hard, steady stare straight into Derek's own eyes as if trying to look into his head.

"Boy... did you say... Turnip Knight?" Not a single blink, Neek continued to eye up Derek.

"Y... yup." Derek felt almost as if the energy from his body was being sucked out of him through Neek's hard stare. His knees began to shake and he couldn't help but to keep staring back at the beaten up knight.

Neek let out a small snigger. Then another. And another. Then, without warning the eye contact that Neek held to Derek was broken and Neek howled and laughed uncontrollably.

"Turnip Knight? Ha! I thought that tale died out back when I was a kid! Thanks a lot lad, that's just made my day!"

Derek's jaw dropped, nearly to the ground, as he looked on in disbelief of Neek and the other knights. Some of the other townsfolk themselves that saw and heard everything were laughing as well.

Derek didn't utter a word on the way home to Doko Village that evening.

VII

Monday morning came quickly after the events of the weekend and Derek was back to his usual self and his usual training routine. Considering the events of the weekend, his morning training went well and he was in good spirits thinking about telling Pippie about the homecoming parade.

"We were near the front so it took ages to properly see it, but they stopped and the King was talking and everything right where we were."

"Derek… it's called 'addressing'… he formally 'addressed' Neek and invited him back to the castle."

"No, I didn't see the king give him any clothes."

"What?" Pippie sighed. "Anyway, have you seen the newspapers today?"

"You know I don't bother with any of that stuff. Why? Was I in it?"

"No. Apparently there's more evidence that there's a dragon living near the village."

"Cool. I hope I get to see it."

"Yeah it'll be the last thing you see before it eats you. But something else happened as well that's pretty important."

"Oh? What?"

"Sir Neek resigned from his position yesterday."

Derek stopped walking for a moment and tried to take in what he was told. One of the most well-known knights of the Zeehan Kingdom had left.

"What? Why?" Derek focussed hard on Pippie, waiting on the answer.

"Don't know. No one outside the castle seems to know. Only the people in the court room at the time would have heard what was given as a reason to the king. But apparently a spokesperson for the king said that there wasn't any reason given. He just up and walked."

"Isn't that a bit strange?"

"Strange? Derek, it's unheard of!"

Derek couldn't shake what Pippie had told him for the rest of the day. What mission did Neek go on and why did he suddenly leave?

Derek was eager to tell his mum as he returned home in the early evening. He drew in a breath as he opened his front door, ready to engage his mother in conversation about the knight. Derek talked to his mum about Neek resigning all the way through dinner and right up until he was in bed and ready to sleep. He realised, just as he was drifting off, that to talk for that long about it, he must have repeated himself at least once.

VIII

Weeks went past and everything in and around Doko Village was normal. Nothing had changed around Derek's training route, or his education, the men were still working the same as they did and talk of Neek fizzled out as it became part of yesterday's news in the somewhat isolated village.

It was Wednesday, early morning, and Derek was getting quite serious with the practice tree. The tree was roughly a 30-minute-walk from the bottom of Dragon's Peak and easily visible even through the trees due to the height of the mountain. As a mountain, it was relatively small, and Derek assumed it was easy to walk up for a Turnip Knight in training, but compared to the small village and farmland of the surrounding area, Dragon's Peak was a towering spectacle, one that even the ancients were said to worship.

If what Pippie was saying about a dragon living up there was true, Derek was well within range to become a snack for one. But that probably wasn't happening.

Derek began to walk back home. While making his way along the muddy road on the outskirts of the village, he realised that this morning wasn't a normal one at all. In between the houses, he could just about make out a crowd gathering in the village centre. As far as Derek could remember, there wasn't any kind of party or festival that was happening today either. Doko Village is founded on its principle of routine, so for everyone to be doing something different there must be something very serious happening.

Derek ran as fast as his legs could carry towards the crowd. As he neared the outside of the congregation, he darted to the left and began to climb the nearest home that rather conveniently had crates stacked up just high enough for Derek to reach the roof. As he reached the top, he heard a nasally, posh, toffee nosed voice call everyone to quiet down. Derek scanned the audience and identified the majority of the village's occupants there. He focussed in on the centre, where a tall, thin knight wearing full armour and bearing the mark of Zeehan stood. He had a thin face, long knobbly chin and an upward turned nose which pointed practically straight up. From how high he held his head he could have looked down his nose and seen the birds flying through the blue skies above. The knight began to talk again.

"Listen to me now, peasants of Doko Village. I am the noble Sir Beef Stroganoff of the Zeehan Kingdom and most trusted knight to the King."

His voice was near unbearable to listen to, his snobbishness wore on Derek's nerves, and he sounded as if a lump of butter was churning around the back of his throat.

"I come bearing urgent news that you must take heed to immediately. Through research that I myself have lead into the surroundings of Dragon's Peak and the nearby forestation, it is clear to us that there has been dragon activity taking place there."

Though it was delivered by what must have been the single worst human being alive, Derek's heart pounded hard against his chest and his eyes widened. A dragon. Here, in Doko Village. Though dragons were notoriously dangerous, he couldn't help getting extremely excited. The irritating knight continued.

"With this in mind, the most noble and gracious King that rules over you and your... rustic village... has decided that it would be in your best interests to know beforehand that as of next week I will begin taking the fight directly to said dragon with the intention of slaying it and returning peace to your simple – I mean, rural – lives."

By now, the villagers had begun to unsettle and the whispers that started a few moments ago became obvious conversations of fear and panic. Husbands grabbed their wives, wives grabbed their children, and children clung to their parent's leg. From the distance, Derek could no longer hear the words that were coming from the repulsive Sir Beef. Derek heard a clunk behind him. Startled, he spun around in a pouncing stance; hand on sword, to see the familiar sight of bright blonde hair. And under the fringe, his friend Pippie.

IX

"Who is that guy, Pip?"

"Sir Beef Stroganoff, he's a knight from Zeehan. He's well known for being stuck up and looking down on folk from the villages."

"When did he get here?"

"About an hour ago. He came on his own horse and started calling the villagers in straight away. Whenever anyone asked why he just said 'because it's the will of your King'."

"You know when he said there was a dragon at Dragon's Peak; did he say anything about what kind or anything? Everyone got too loud so I couldn't hear."

"I came up here as soon as I saw you, didn't hear anything. Sorry."

The crowd began to quieten down and Sir Beef continued talking.

"… quieten down please over there, thank you. The next week will be very crucial for me as I prepare to take on the wretched beast. As of this day next week, my personal unit will be taking post around Doko Village to keep watch. I'm afraid your village will be locked down at that time."

"And what about our work? How the hell am I supposed to tend my crops if you lock down the village? My fields are to the West and Dragon's Peak is in the East, I'm not even putting myself in danger." A farmer in the crowd spoke up. The rest of the villagers looked at each other in agreement. Sir Beef replied:

"Know that it is to keep intruders out, not you in. You will have to find other things to do with your time."

"Other things to do with my time? I have to tend those crops to live you stupid fool, I don't do it because I ploughin' feel like it!"

Sir Beef's eyes narrowed in on the man, and he drew his eye lids in to a glare. "Mind who you're talking to, peasant, I could have a lowly servant to our king cut down for less foul language than that in front of an esteemed elite such as myself. Speak again, and I'll not hesitate to cut your head off."

The man drew back a couple steps, fear striking his face. The rest of the crowd seemed to do the same, giving the arrogant knight a wider circle. Derek felt butterflies in his stomach and a sick feeling in his throat. This wasn't wooden swords or practice trees; this man was a real soldier and could really hurt someone for real. Though Derek had trained hard this past year, he knew he was still a long way from being able to take on someone like Sir Beef.

The crowd parted as Sir Beef walked back towards the village gates where he'd left his horse. He walked with his chin high and a smug grin on his face, as if he took pleasure from the fear he'd put into the villagers. As he walked towards the hut, Derek and Pippie watched him from, he told the horror struck crowd that he and his men would return next week to secure Doko Village. He walked under the hut where Derek and Pippie stood. Derek glared at Sir Beef, wishing to be able to do something to wipe the smug look off his face.

Suddenly, a small stone pelted towards Sir Beef's head, narrowly missing him by millimetres. Derek, wondering if his mere thought was what caused it; he looked around bewildered to see Pippie lying flat on his stomach trying to hide.

Derek, knowing Doko Village inside out, realised that Sir Beef wasn't going the fastest way to the village gate where his horse is. With a small jerk of the neck, signalling Pippie to follow, they clambered down from the hut and rushed off towards the town gate before any of the adults could call them back.

"Where are we going?" Asked Pippie, as he huffed and puffed to keep up with Derek.

"Let's give that arrogant sod a leaving present."

Before too long, they made it to the village gate. There, just outside, and out of the way of any of the locals' horses, was the well-groomed steed ridden by Sir Beef. Derek and Pippie ran quickly to the gate and checked the direction that Sir Beef would be coming from before stepping out of the village walls and towards the horses. With Pippie keeping watch, Derek began moving handfuls of horse manure from the pile a few metres away, into the saddlebag of Sir Beef's horse. Pippie got Derek's attention:

"Derek… Derek… I can see him, hurry up. What are you doing anyway?"

"Sssshhhhh, just stall him a bit."

Pippie panicked and looked around for something to improvise with. Finding nothing, he disappeared around the corner and headed towards Sir Beef. Not having time to wonder what Pippie was doing or if he'd be okay, Derek carried on with his master plan.

Derek could hear the nasal noise of Sir Beef's voice getting closer and closer to the village gates. He quickly dived over the low wall and behind a hay stack, turning just in time to see the tall Sir Beef walking around the corner. Almost at the same time, nearly startling Derek enough to make him squeal, Pippie appeared next to Derek, looking over his shoulder to see what dastardly deeds Derek had conjured up.

With his chin so high and mighty, Sir Beef didn't notice the excess manure packed into the saddle bag of his royal steed. He untied the horse, still oblivious, and lined up to mount it. He got a foot on the saddle hold okay and threw his body up, successfully sitting atop the royal horse. Grasping at the manes he whipped the horse to rear up. Sniggering, Derek and Pippie watched as the horse galloped off down the road stinking of poop. Derek and Pip howled with laughter as they watched Sir Beef disappear down the road.

X

Derek returned home to a clip around the ear from Mother. "In this time of crisis," she says, "I want to keep an eye on you, Delly."

Emergency measures were being taken by villagers all through the day after the arrival of Sir Beef. Men that worked the crops were trying to move as much of their produce inside the village walls in any pot they could find, diamond hunters were working triple fold trying to find enough to make up for the coming week off. And most importantly, school was out.

Derek, without anything to do, managed to convince Pippie to go with him to the practice tree in the afternoon. Pippie wasn't much good with a sword, so he mainly just watched.

"*Hi ya!* So if this guy comes over, *ooft,* and finds no actual dragons, *ha,* what happens? Does he just go home?"

"He'll probably get angry, maybe kick over a haystack, and go home."

"And if there is, *ayah,* what'll he do to it?"

"Well, he'll try and kill it." Derek stopped and looked at Pippie.

"But dragons are rare, right? I thought completely ending animals was bad?"

"Ending? You mean extinct, Derek."

"What? Who's extinct?"

"No, you *mean* extinct."

"About what?"

"Dragons."

"No you got it wrong, dragons aren't extinct, we might have one over there." Pippie glared at Derek for a few seconds, and turned away to finish his daisy chain.

Derek churned everything over in his head while attacking the defenceless tree. There could be a dragon living not an hour's walk away from where he was up the mountain. A dragon, a rare animal in this day and age, could be sitting around and someone was planning to come and take that away without anyone seeing it alive. If Beef did find a dragon on Dragon's Peak, Derek would be lucky to even see the body.

Derek and Pippie began the walk back to the village. They crossed the rope bridge, looking down and around in the open ravine. The waterfall crashed against the rocks, thick branches hung out from the 90 degree drop, bugs gathered around flowers to collect the pollen, and a hooded figure sat still against the rocks. Realising what he saw just as he finished crossing the rope bridge, Derek doubled back to check he saw that right.

Peering over the edge covered by the pole at the end of the bridge, Derek could see a lone figure in a full length hooded robe sat against the rocks a short way down stream.

"Derek what are you do…" Derek cut Pippie short with a hand over the mouth.

"… Shhh." Derek nodded his head in the direction of the hooded figure. Pippie cottoned on, and they crept to the edge of the bridge to look. Pippie whispered to Derek:

"You come here a lot, right? Are there usually other people hanging around?"

"No. Not that I've ever seen."

"I can't quite make out who it is."

"Me neither, you think it's human?"

"Well yeah, sub-human creatures don't generally live around here. The only time Elves ever come here is for royal visits."

"You think it could be a royal elf then?"

"What the hell would a royal elf be doing sitting by the river, hood up, on a sunny day like this? Obviously it's someone that doesn't want to be seen, someone laying low."

Pippie convinced Derek to leave and they headed back to Doko Village. Derek, however, was still interested in who the man was, long into the evening.

XI

Two o'clock in the morning, and Derek was sound asleep in his bed. A full moon was beaming an enchanting white light into his room. The bars of light coming in through the window were suddenly disturbed. A human-shape figure eclipsed the illumination, its shape had imprinted on the bedroom floor as it began moving into the room.

Quickly, a hand cupped Derek's mouth. Derek stayed asleep, the whistling of his nose increased as he drew all his breath through his nostrils. The other hand of the shadowy invader pinched at Derek's nose, stopping him from breathing entirely. Before too long, Derek awoke with an almighty gasp.

Now awake, Derek could see the dark figure lying over him on his bed, his eyes shot open wide in fear and he wondered what he could do. His sword and other Turnip Knight training armour was on the other side of the room (he kept meaning to practice sleeping with his sword under his bed but it always slipped his mind). Derek turned back to look at the face of the shadowy figure. Through the brightness of the moonlight, he could see it had blonde hair, and before long, realised this person must have been around his size.

With the second hand of the shadowy figure now away from Derek's nose, the face of Pippie slowly moved towards

Derek and into the light coming through the window. As he moved into view, he put his forefinger to his mouth and let out a little "Shhhh" to keep Derek from making noise. Pippie got off Derek and removed his hand from his mouth. Derek sat up.

"Pip? What the hell?"

"I've been thinking about that person we saw down by the waterfall."

"Yeah, well I was dreaming about riding a Galgazar up to the peak of a demonic castle and saving Princess Agosteen and winning her heart."

"Princess Agosteen is at least fourteen, she's way too old for you."

"Yeah well it was a dream and it was awesome. Why are you here anyway?"

"Like I said, I was thinking about that guy – thing – and I want to go and see if he – it – is still there."

"What... *now*? Are you insane? What if my mum wakes up? Have you ever been hit by her kitchen stuff..."

"... Utensils..."

"... what did you call me? Anyway, yeah, it really hurts. If I go sneaking out into the woods at this time and die, she'll kill me."

"I thought you were some brave hero or something?"

"I'm *in training*; I'm not quite a hero yet."

"Well wouldn't a Turnip Knight in training be fearless enough to go out and adventure? You want to be a big hero, you have to take a big risk sooner or later you can't just keep hitting a tree for the rest of your life."

Derek thought about it for a moment. "Ugh, fine, let me just grab my stuff and put some clothes on."

Derek, now fully equipped with his Turnip Knight in training gear, jumped out through the window and set off for Bikhin Forest with Pippie. Because of the amount of work everyone had been doing in the lead up to Sir Beef occupying and locking down the village, all the villagers were working extra hard and none seemed to be awake. Taking advantage of that, Derek and Pippie easily made it to Bikhin Forest without anybody seeing or hearing them.

As they approached, Derek and Pippie couldn't see a single tree past the ones on the edge of the forest. The forest was pitch black. Getting to the forest was well lit thanks to the full moon, but next to no light was getting in past the thick foliage.

Derek and Pippie looked at each other, both with an equally terrified look on their faces.

"How are we going to see anything in there?" Derek asked his companion.

"Don't worry, once we're in there our eyes will adjust and we'll be able to see just fine."

"Just fine? Are you being serious?"

"Okay… well we'll be able to see where we're going at least."

"And what happens if we come across monsters in there? It's the night; encounters are a lot more likely than they are in the day. And we all know there are goblins in there."

"What the hell was all that training for if you can't at least stand up to a bloody goblin?"

"Goblins are real monsters you know, they attack people."

"Yeah, and literally everyone can beat a goblin."

"Bet you can't beat a goblin."

"I'm not a grown up."

39

"But I'm not a grown up either, we're the same age, remember?"

"Yeah but you still have a weapon. So if we come across a goblin you have to fight it."

"Fine. Have my sword."

"I don't know how to use it. Stop being a coward, you'll level up loads from this, I guarantee."

Each twig snapping step they took led them closer to the pitch black darkness of the forest. Getting to this point seemed to happen almost instantly but these last few steps felt like a lifetime. Finally, Derek touched the first tree and leaned his head into the darkness. He and Pippie were now officially inside Bikhin Forest. A far more dangerous forest in the night than in the day.

Some monsters of the world, classified in the Official Adventurers Encyclopaedia, seemed to make a habit out of attacking people that come across them. That's most likely what makes them classified as 'dangerous monsters'. Monsters are different from animals in that they can sometimes possess weapons such as knives and swords, or even use magic. Normal animals, like rabbits, don't do that. When an adventurer is out in the field, he/she is more likely to come across a monster in the night. That has been known since before adventuring officially became an occupation. Famous adventurer and author of the first edition of the Official Adventurers Encyclopaedia, Donoldan Dicklebury, is well known for his quote: "The modern adventurer should expect to find weapon wielding goblins, but not a rabbit with a knife. That would be a peculiar sight, indeed."

Derek, wanting to become someone that would travel a lot, knows this all too well.

Derek could barely see anything. Next to him, he could hear the footsteps of his partner and feel his hand on Derek's shoulder. Together they walked, slowly, deeper into the forest towards the rope bridge. Luckily Derek had walked the path hundreds of times since he began training and could get there with his eyes closed, which was a good thing because there was so little light he may as well have done just that. Either that or he was so scared he did have his eyes shut and didn't realise.

In the distance Derek could see the occasional glow of what could have been eyes staring him down. The dim moonlight that made it through the thick brush occasionally flickered in the distance as if something eclipsed the light; the only thing Derek wanted to know was what exactly that something was…

After what felt like hours in the darkness, they finally found the opening in the trees, the noisy waterfall, and the safe rope bridge. The moonlight illuminated the opening a lot better here without the trees getting in the way, and now Derek and Pippie could see properly once again.

"See, that wasn't so bad, was it."

After Pippie spoke, a silhouette from within the darkness began to move towards them.

"Why'd you have to say that, Pip."

XII

The silhouette gingerly made its way towards the opening where Derek and Pippie stood. Derek felt his heart pounding; it was going so hard, he thought it was in his head. He looked at Pippie wondering if he could hear it as well. The silhouette dodged and dashed in and out from behind the trees as it made its way closer.

Derek gripped his sword tightly, his breathing got heavier and faster and his heart continued to beat louder and louder. It pumped so hard now in his ear he could hardly hear the forest floor crack and snap as the unidentified silhouette continued to close in.

The approaching silhouette now stood behind the last tree before the clearing. From behind the shadows, three long, green, bony fingers wrapped themselves around the trunk of the tree. The face, that until now only had two glowing eyes, now showed a large knobbly nose and long crooked chin. Finally, the rest of the head came forward into the moonlight. The face was littered with boils, though still green, and so thin that the bones of the cheeks stood out like doorknobs. The hair was long, mangy and clumped up behind the pointy ears that each had a fairly impressive pile of hair coming out from the middle. Derek stood petrified. This was his first time seeing a goblin. A fully grown adult male goblin.

The eyes of the goblin narrowed in and he smiled, revealing his black and yellow teeth, all five of them. His mouth opened and a dark red tongue fell out. He breathed out heavily, making a snarling sound as he did so. Derek breathed through his nose as his mouth stayed bolted shut, his jaw trembling in fear.

The wild goblin walked out from behind the tree; revealing his scraggy clothes, and stood with his knees bent out sideways (this was normal for a goblin). In the hand they hadn't seen yet, the goblin held a fairly large club (about three quarters the size or Derek) that got thicker the further up it got. On the end of the club, where it was as big around as Derek's head, countless rusty nails stuck out at jagged angles.

The fear rooted Derek firmly to the ground and petrified his body. He stood as a statue. He wanted to turn to see if Pippie was still behind, to check another goblin hadn't sneaked behind and captured him, but he couldn't move. He couldn't even blink. He was worried that if he blinked, the goblin might attack him.

The smell of the goblin was unspeakable. A mix of sweat, dirty socks, rotten meat and damp wood. His glowing yellow eyes looked Derek up and down, and he made another sniggering noise. He raised his large club up over his shoulder and the long disgusting tongue licked around his face, passing right up just under his eyes, and curling under his chin, leaving a bit of yellow spit smeared across his neck. The lick also passed over his many boils, opening one up. Derek watched as the contents seeped out and ran down his face.

In horror of the creature, Derek's body began to move. His legs took a step back, seemingly by themselves, and he placed the palm of his hand over his mouth. With his mouth muted, he let out a gentle weep. Although he tried to hide the noise, the goblin seemed to hear it, and took a step closer with a snigger. From the unknown behind him, Derek heard Pippie's voice.

"Derek, you have to do something." Derek turned his eyes away from the disgusting creature and looked at Pippie. Pippie stared back at him; with tears building, he lipped the words, "Do something."

Derek turned back to face the goblin, took a deep breath and tried to take in the situation. They were miles from home, miles from safety, and if Derek did nothing, then he and Pippie wouldn't see tomorrow.

The goblin crept nearer and nearer. With every step, Derek's heart beat grew louder and louder. What could he do? He only had a little wooden sword, compared to the nailed club, it wasn't much. Behind him, he could hear his scared friend draw back away from the goblin. Derek was scared out of his mind, but he had to do something. The goblin had crept to within a metre of Derek now, and Derek could feel the musty breath punching at his nostrils.

Before Derek knew what was going on, the goblin grabbed his massive club with his other hand and swung vertically at Derek's head. Pippie screamed, the club hurled towards Derek, the tip of the nails sparkling in the moonlight. As if in slow motion, Derek saw what might end his life hurtling towards him. With all the strength he could muster, he vaulted himself out the way to the left, landing on the forest floor.

The club pounded into the ground, muddy dust flying out from the epicentre of the strike. Derek stood as quickly as he could, breathing fast and heavy. Before he had the chance to catch his breath the goblin furiously yanked the club out from the ground, soft mud covered the nails that penetrated the forest floor. The goblin stepped and swung again, this time horizontally but still aiming to take Derek's head off. Derek hit the ground, allowing the club to pass over him, but one of the nails caught the top of his wooden helmet, his head pelted to the left and he hit the ground again. The wooden hat flew off into the distance and Derek lay slightly dazed. He got to his hands and knees in time to hear his friend shout, "LOOK OUT!" Before Derek could look up to see what was coming, a ghastly green goblin shin had kicked him in the ribs.

XIII

Derek hurtled through the air and hit the ground not far from Pippie. The pain was immense. Derek stayed on the floor, rolled up in a ball, clutching at his side. Pippie's hands rocked the fallen hero as he pleaded with him to get up. Those pleads became a yelp, as the goblin picked Pippie up by his head.

Pippie struggled, twisted and shouted, trying desperately to get free from the clutches of the wild goblin. Derek winced and wheezed as he squeezed his eyes shut. He had to think fast… what can he do? He looked up to see it staring at Pippie, looking very pleased with itself. He shut his eyes again and thought hard.

All he could think was how much he wanted the goblin to go away, how much he wanted it to leave him and Pippie alone. He felt a burning in his chest, and he kept on thinking about wanting the goblin gone. He looked up at the goblin again, in his mind shouting, "GO AWAY, GO AWAY, GO AWAY." The goblin looked confused for a moment, and then looked down at Derek, acknowledging him for the first time since it picked Pippie up.

The goblin dropped Pippie to the ground, who was also now looking at Derek. Derek continued to think and imagine the goblin going away, wanting it gone. The burning in his chest grew and grew as he thought, 'go away, go away,' over and over. He gained the strength to stand, so he did and the goblin stepped back, still confused. The burning in Derek's chest grew hotter and hotter; all fear became anger and hate. He clenched his fist tight.

The burning in Derek's chest continued to grow. The burning feeling began to move, heating up his shoulder, then the arm, and finally to his clenched fist. Derek's hand, burning like it was set alight, started to glow. The glowing grew brighter, and still brighter, bright white light lit the forest casting shadows of the goblin and Pippie against the trees and mud.

Like a lightning bolt, Derek was thrust forward fist first and straight into the wild goblin. Derek's fist sunk into the pot belly of the goblin, the bright light in Derek's fist exploded on impact and the goblin was launched, butt-first, off his feet and onto the forest floor, metres away.

Derek looked at his hand and then at the goblin heaped on the floor, unmoving. A few green fingers twitched, and then the injured goblin finally raised its surprised head. It scrabbled around and got back to his feet before taking a few paces back. The goblin breathed heavily, staring at Derek and looking very confused with what just happened.

It could have been fear, it could have been confusion, but for whatever reason, the goblin backed away towards the dark of the woods. As it turned to disappear into the night, Derek noticed the shadowy figure behind it, lurking around in the dimness of the trees. Before the goblin had even noticed the dark figure, it struck the goblin with a single swing of the arm. The goblin flew into the air like a beetle being flicked off a table, but as it left the ground, it seemed to burst into flames and within a couple of seconds was completely gone.

Derek, still taken aback by how he hit the goblin, focussed in on the potential new enemy. Pippie lay still where he was dropped, also struggling to take in everything that was happening. The dark figure walked forwards towards Derek and Pippie, revealing himself to be a man under a long cloak. A deep, commanding voice came from under the hood. "That was quite the spell you just cast there boy, you don't look like you study magic, so I'm impressed."

Derek took a foot back, prepared to move or dodge or run. This man had incinerated the goblin that nearly killed him and Pippie with a single hit of his hand, he knew there was no way he could fight him. The cloaked man walked forwards more, drawing closer to the two boys. "Casting Exploding Light in your situation – or without training for that matter – is no easy feat. Well done to you indeed, boy."

He walked closer, but then, although Derek was clearly the one with the amazing punching skills, the man swerved towards Pippie. The cloaked man knelt down, and helped Pippie up slowly. "C'mon, find your footing, using spells can take it out of you if you don't have the magic power for it."

Derek, bewildered, spoke up. "Hey, I don't know if it was because it was dark or something, but you know it was me that hit that goblin with the punch y'know."

"I could see it all very clearly little boy, though you were the one that did the attacking, your friend here is the one that cast Exploding Light. He cast it on you."

Pippie then perked up. "I cast Exploding Light on Derek?"

"Yes. To be honest you're both very lucky, when you cast it something wasn't right, it could have happened a lot sooner but the spell took some time to take effect. You're lucky you didn't do damage to your friend."

"I felt a burning in my chest, then it moved along my arm and into my hand."

"Exploding Light was cast on your chest and you converted it to your fist? I've never heard of anyone manipulating someone else's magic like that before."

"Hear that Pip, we're basically the best team ever."

"Shut up Derek."

XIV

The thrills of the night calmed down somewhat since the cloaked man came and rescued Derek and Pippie from the wild goblin. According the cloaked man, Pippie had managed to cast a magic spell called Exploding Light on Derek, enabling him to hit the goblin with a bit of force, although somehow Pippie cast it on Derek's chest and Derek was able to move the magic energy to his hand. Derek decided it was time to get some answers from the cloaked man.

"So who are you anyway?"

"Derek, be quiet. Hello sir, my name is Pip and this is Derek. And what might your name be?"

"I think young Derek here might be able to tell you." The cloaked man removed his hood, revealing his middle aged, rugged face.

"Huh?" Derek stared at the man for a moment, trying to work out who he was. "Nope. Don't know you. Sorry."

"Derek, oh my gosh, don't you know who this is?" Pippie then chimed in.

"Nope. I thought it might be my dad for a moment but I'm pretty sure he doesn't look like this guy."

"Young man, you saw me only a few weeks ago, how can you not remember who I am?"

"I saw a lot of people a few weeks ago mate."

"You so did not, Derek." Pippie chimed in.

"Shut up Pip. Look can you just tell me who you are now? Please?"

"That, Derek, is Sir Burten Neek."

"Who?"

"Holy… it's the man you saw in Zeehan returning to the castle a few weeks ago you moron!"

Derek narrowed his eyes on Neek for a moment once again, and then it clicked.

Neek sat back on the forest floor. Derek remembered Pippie telling him how Neek left his position as a Zeehan Sir and disappeared not long after returning from his previous mission.

"Why are you here, then?" Derek continued the conversation with a very clear question.

"After stepping away from my role at the palace, I needed to escape the boundaries and many eyes of the city. I have been moving around this area ever since."

"Sir, do you also sleep out here?" Pippie now was also interested to know more, but far more polite.

"Yes, although it can be dangerous it's fair to say that the creatures around here can sense not to approach me."

"So what happened anyway Sir Neek? Why did you leave, might I ask?" Pippie persisted with manners.

"Or were you booted out?" Derek persisted, without manners.

"Derek! What he means is… we'd like to know exactly what happened."

"Pip reckons there's more going on, but you looked pretty beaten up at the parade. And you laughed at me! You might have probably just saved our lives but you have some explaining to do."

"I think what Derek means is that you definitely saved our lives and thank you for that. Wait, did you say he laughed at you?"

"Yeah, he and some posh looking goon laughed at me for wanting to be a Turnip Knight."

Finally, Neek was able to speak.

"I see there are many questions. Usually I wouldn't bother to explain myself to children, but I see you two are exceptional in some way or another. So I will explain. But please, no more interrupting and no more talking. You have one mouth and two ears; you must now listen for double the time you have spoken."

"I apologise for laughing young man, but you see there is no such thing as a Turnip Knight. It was originally an old tale told to young kids to get them to eat their turnips, as turnips are good for you but not always the nicest thing to eat. As for the dragon, I do not know for sure if there is a dragon currently on Dragon's Peak. I have indeed been tracking a dragon, but the trace went cold some time ago and I returned home."

"As you saw, Derek, my armour was beaten and I was soundly defeated in keeping up with the creature I was tracking. Originally, I was tracking some kind of combatant, an adventurer or warrior of some sort, and that led me to the dragon that I believe the combatant is the tamer. This combatant had at his disposal a very powerful creature, and I now fear after coming back home that Sir Beef wants to take control of that dragon for himself. I don't trust the snivelling little rat; I don't believe his intentions are pure. You see Sir Beef is not as great with a sword as I am, but he instead possesses the skills and knowledge of runes and other magic. This talent he has makes him very efficient at taking control of powerful creatures. Maybe even a dragon. A dragon is still to this day the only creature that there has been no documented proof of anyone successfully controlling. That's what made this dragon and this unknown combatant so interesting."

Neek, Derek and Pippie stayed there at the opening for what seemed like hours. Neek explained to the boys that he was tracking the dragon and hoping to get to it before Beef does. He didn't know exactly what kind of dragon it was but the dragon had been the reason he left the kingdom. Neek had been tracking an unknown warrior who seemed to have the ability to control a very powerful dragon. When he finally got close to the target in Daburan, the dragon just disappeared and along with it, the warrior he was tracking.

"Only one thing was the same about the warrior everywhere I travelled," Neek explained, "everyone that saw the warrior always called him the same thing. They all said he was the Sky Paladin."

XV

Neek walked the two young adventurers back to Doko Village. It wasn't long until day break and the boys needed to get back to bed quickly so their parents didn't know they were gone. Neek left them at the village gate and returned to the forest. Before leaving, he warned them to be weary of Sir Beef; although he was a horrible old git on the surface, Beef was in fact a very powerful warrior and extremely dangerous when angry. "He may not draw a sword and cut you down, but he's very skilled and his manipulative magic through the use of runes could get into your head." After Neek's warning, he returned to the forest.

Derek made it back into bed just before morning; he was due to wake up in under an hour by the time his head hit the pillow, and although he planned to be up on time to keep his mum from getting suspicious, he was out like a light until midday. With no school due to the mass panic and only six days until the village lock down, Derek's mum was happy that he was asleep and out of the way while she and the rest of the villagers made the preparations for the lock down.

It was lunch time when Derek finally woke up. Although still a bit tired and drained from the events of the previous night, he panicked when he realised he missed his usual wake up time. After finishing his lunch he went to meet up with Pippie again, who was also asleep until lunch time.

"Mum didn't mind that I didn't get up for training this morning, said I deserved a break."

"That's lucky. My mum thinks I was awake because of the warm Yeastling I ate last night."

"What's a Yeastling?"

"You've never had a Yeastling? It's like a little bun but really really sweet with a caramel topping."

"Oh, yeah I think I saw those in Zeehan the other week, are they good?"

"They're amazing! But I don't have them often, they're a treat. But I won't be getting them before bed any more. Thanks for that by the way."

"Hey it isn't my fault, you're the one that went all Spectrephage and came into my room at the dead of night."

"Sssshhhhh, someone might hear you. You know Beef's knights are already hanging around here."

"Really? I haven't seen any. What are they wearing?"

A Zeehan knight wearing a shimmering chest plate bearing the Zeehan crest with green etchings (the colour of Sir Beef's division), a huge sword attached to his golden holster and heavy thumping boots noisily came around the corner and passed Pippie and Derek, giving them a cold glance and a rough grunt as he walked past. They heard him as he walked on around the corner, and long into the distance, before his noise was finally drowned out by the busy-body villagers packing and preparing.

Derek looked at Pippie. "Well, that was just bad timing."

XVI

A few days pass in Doko village with Derek getting as much training in as he can at the practice tree before the village-wide lock down. With no school and the newspapers from Zeehan stopped, Pippie found himself with very little to do and tagged along with Derek during his training, all the while trying desperately to cast Exploding Light. The last and only time he managed to cast the spell was during their encounter with the goblin in the woods the night they met Neek.

It was mid-morning, and Derek was making his way back to the village from the practice tree. He made his way through Bikhin forest, his eyes unable to adjust to the constant switch between shadow and sun under the thickness of the trees. In the distance, amongst the rustling of the leaves and creaking of branches in the wind, faint voices could be heard.

Derek slowed down his advance and crept closer to the voices, tree by tree, using them as cover. He crept and pursued, when suddenly, his foot got caught, tripping him over and putting him face first into a barky face-plant of his intended cover. His face connected with the tree, disorientating him as he struggled to recover his balance and keep hidden. The pain of the hit took his hearing and sight for a split second, he managed to stumble and keep his footing.

He came to, and pressed himself against the tree, panting heavily.

He slowed his breathing and strained his ears to hear the voices over the pounding of his heartbeat. As he calmed down, the voices came back. 'Got away with that one then,' he thought to himself.

Peering around the cover of the tree, Derek made out two figures in the distance. One was tall and broad, draped in a long coat and hooded. The other was thin and weaselly, with a distinguishable pointed chin and nose high in the air. Burten Neek and Sir Beef Stroganoff.

Derek strained his ears and concentrated hard to listen to the conversation. He couldn't be sure if the conversation was heated, the knight and former knight didn't seem to be fighting and neither were they shouting. Derek was in luck as the wind whisked between the trees from their conversation towards him, carrying the sound of their voices with it.

"… you have no idea what you're getting yourself into, Beef."

"Might I remind you that I am still a Sir under the command of the illustrious king and you should address me appropriately."

"Just cut that crap for a minute and listen to me. I know we never saw eye to eye, but this is different. The person I was tracking, the Sky Paladin, it all links back to whatever is in that cave."

"Well I suppose any information at this time might help in preparation for when I finally find the beast. Speak on, Neek, but beware my patience is short for traitors of the kingdom."

"That creature in that cave is the familiar of the Sky Paladin. I tracked him for over eight months, from here to

Al'Heal'the, and it made its way back here in a matter of days. You know no normal creature can travel as far as the capital of the Higher Elves and back in one day, not without incredible power."

"Did you mark sightings of the beast a day before the first log was submitted to the council about it being here? Or is the fact that it made its way across the entirety of the Northern Realm without the use of a portal just you guessing?"

"No, I didn't see it but-"

"… but nothing, Neek. Your information is useless. Your mission was a complete failure and you have returned mad. The king should have just ordered you hanged out of respect for your once esteemed name."

Sir Beef stood closer to Neek, looking him in the eyes. Sir Beef's thin face and piercing eyes contrasted against Neek's bruised, rugged face and slightly hazed eyes.

"I won't let you get at that creature, Beef. It's a lot more powerful than you realise and you'll never get out alive."

"What do you intend to do, Neek? You have been stripped of your armour, your master-crafted weapon; you are but a man in a cloak making idle threats to a royal guard. Get in my way, Neek, and it'll be treason to the highest degree and that means death. So I suggest you scurry off back under your hole and let a real knight do his job. I have your hair, Neek, and you know my skills with runes. By this time tomorrow, you will not be able to enter within a mile of that filthy village or the cave."

"Wait, where did you get my hair?"

"Beside the point, my dear man. Now, you have your warning, so spend the rest of the day preparing and get out of my sight. For good."

The two men stood, staring each other down. Neek breathed heavily through his nostrils. Both men's eyes continued to fix themselves into each other like a staring contest, neither blinking nor either moving. Finally, Neek gave a heavy exhale and shook his head. "You won't listen to me, Beef. Fine. Good luck to you."

With that closing comment, Neek turned towards Derek and marched away, leaving the slim, smug knight behind him. Derek, forgetting himself from being caught up in the argument, wasn't prepared for Neek marching towards him and didn't even consider making himself hidden until Neek was within a metre of him. Derek panicked and probably caused more noise than if he had just stood still as Neek closed in towards him. "I've known you were there all along, boy. Come with me, we need to talk."

XVII

"Beef has gone; I am sorry that I lied to you."

"Lied? What?"

"You listened to the conversation?"

"Yeah."

"So you heard me talk about the dragon on Dragon's Peak?"

"Yeah. Wait, did you say before you didn't think there was one?"

"Do you ever pay attention, young man?"

Another voice, the voice of Pippie, came from the direction of the village. "I was listening, Sir Neek."

"Oh hey Pip, what you doing out here?"

"You left me behind, you idiot, I was waiting for you. Anyway, Sir Neek what's all this about you lying?"

"Ah, yes, well... you see... there is indeed almost certainly a dragon on Dragon's Peak."

"I bloody well knew it! Ha, suck it, Pip!" Derek threw up his arms in celebration.

"Yes young man, you were correct. Considering your ability to listen and hold information I am impressed by your natural intuition." Derek was too busy praising himself to hear what Neek just said.

"I told you the lie to protect you both. This dragon is surely the most powerful creature I have ever come across, potentially as powerful as the legendary Turtle-dera-dora."

"The who-what-now?"

"Damn it Derek! Read a newspaper for once in your life! The Turtle-dera-dora was a humongous creature that took an almighty team of high level knights, adventurers and beast slayers to defeat. The battle lasted non-stop for over 42 hours, that's two days! How did you not know about that?"

"Ohhhhh yeah, I think I remember you mentioning the big turtle thing. Why did they kill it, again?"

"Sir Neek? Maybe you can explain since you were there and you fought it?"

"Erm, well, y'see, it was very big and someone in the kingdom deemed it very dangerous. It could have potentially flattened the entirety of Doko Village in a single swipe, for example. So it was decided by members of the royal high court that the creature should be removed prior to damage being done."

"So you killed a creature before it did anything?"

"Hey, yeah. Sir Neek, why did you do that?" Pippie now sided with Derek in the questioning.

"I am afraid, my young friends, that there are many things we are commissioned to do by the kingdom that I may not choose to do myself. Not all of the decisions made are in the best interest of the people or of the kingdom, but of individuals looking for personal gain."

"I'm lost. What about the dragon?"

"Haha! Yes young Derek, direct to the point. Apologise for getting side tracked there. The point is that the dragon is extremely powerful, and if Beef is not killed by his attempt to

61

take it as his own, then he may well end up too powerful and not feel like he need serve the kingdom anymore."

"Sir! You really think a distinguished knight could do such a thing?"

"I do, indeed."

Derek sat back and leaned against his palms and looked up to the sky. Greyness swept overhead that day. He closed his eyes to visualise and understand everything he'd just heard. At least one knight of the kingdom, Beef Stroganoff, is a proper toe-rag. Neek is sure there's a dragon with incredible power up in the hills and caves of the Dragon's Peak Mountains. Did they really need to kill the Turtle-dera-dora? 'It would have made a cool familiar when I finally became a Turnip Knight,' he thought to himself. What was Mum cooking for dinner? Whatever it was, Derek was hungry and needed to eat and it was getting really hard to concentrate without something in his belly.

The winds whistled between the trees and the leaves danced to nature's whimsical song. The constant sound of buzzing insects and the beautiful natural songs of the birds that inhabited the trees and bringing them life could be heard between the stronger winds, giving soul and personality to the outback where the three of them sat and talked. The faint light of the sun behind the dull greyness of the sky moved west overhead, signalling the passage of time by which the two boys got more up to speed with the things Neek wanted to tell them.

Derek and Pippie had learned a lot from Neek. They went back to Doko Village with Neek, assuring them he would be around in the area for some time longer to keep tabs on Beef and his intentions. The boys agreed to tell Neek about new developments from within the village; although he didn't tell them how to contact him. He only said that he'll be there when they need him to be.

XVIII

The morning sun rose once again over Dragon's Peak, but this time no blades of light pierced into the mud huts. This time the pitter-patter of rain skipped against the roofs of the mud and wood huts and dripped onto the pile of crates stacked up against the home of Derek; the still-in-training Turnip Knight. Derek launched himself with the ferocity of a small mouse back onto the crates and he began to descend towards the safety of the ground below. The wetness of the wood made it all the more treacherous this morning but Derek was a Turnip Knight in training and he had to be strong and courageous. He reached the second crate down and continued towards the next. Reaching with his left foot, he transferred his weight but the slipperiness of the crate caught him off guard and he lost all footing. Before he could catch himself, in what felt like the blink of an eye, Derek plummeted and hit the floor with a hard thud.

He lay motionless for a moment wondering if he'd broken himself and gasping for breath. The rain hit his face, which he found uncomfortable, so he finally lifted himself up. He looked himself left and right to check for marks and cuts, thankfully he was able to give himself the all clear. Although not the ideal start to the day it did remind him that he should really start to think about learning some first aid, just in case he gets injured while out in the field.

From around the corner, there came the metallic clatter of running armour. Derek looked around in time to see a man dressed head to toe in battle armour and sporting the green marking of Sir Beek Stroganoff as he clumsily clunked his way towards Derek. His face was screwed up and he frowned all the way across his face. He set his eyes on Derek sat on the floor outside his home.

"Oi! You! What the bloody hell you think you're doing around here this early?"

"I live here. I can be here if I want!"

"Don't you go lying to me you little scum bag, I'll have you strung up if you don't start telling the truth!"

"Shhhhhhh. If you wake my mum she'll smash you around the head so hard you'll think its next week." Derek wasn't going to allow himself to be bullied by the man in the armour. He might be part of Sir Beef's forces, but he's not going to tell Derek where he can and can't go in his own home. He was also bluffing a bit; it's more likely his mum will hit him over the head than this knight!

"Oh is that right, is it? Tell you what you little bugger; I'm gonna' take you back to Sir Stroganoff right now and tell him there's a bloomin' thief in the town. A thief operatin' when people are struggling to prepare for a potential dragon attack ain't gonna go down well for you, lad."

Derek gulped. He wasn't sure what else he could do and his mind fixated on himself being sat in jail, wrongly accused and sentenced for being a thief. Before the armour-clad man could grab him the front door to his neighbours home, an older man called Kelderan, opened. Mr Kelderan stepped out in his beige trousers and olive green top. He had a confused look on his face, obviously he had been woken up by the commotion outside and wanted to investigate. He looked at the knight in armour, then at Derek, and then back at the knight. The knight spoke:

"No reason to be alarmed, sir, just caught this little thief in the act that's all."

"That's not a thief you stupid brat, that boy lives there!"

"If you could watch your tone for me please sir, you can't be speakin' to an authority force like that. He's a thief and he'll be tried in court as a thief cus' my word is law 'ere."

"Oh yeah? Well let me tell you a little something about law you nasty little jumped up sod. The law is here to protect the citizens of the kingdom, not so block heads like you with a lust for power can go around bullying little boys." The knight took a step back, startled. "You look at me and think I'm just some stupid old goat, I'll have you know I used to be a top advisor to the king's father! You talk about your power of law well I bloody well wrote them! Now you clear off before we open you like a tin of sardines!"

There was a moment of silence, and of utter astonishment (both from the knight and Derek). Without a word being said, the knight stepped away from Derek. Derek looked around to see Rhadia Flohgan, the lumberjack, also standing there wielding an axe with a head at least the size of Derek's entire body. On the other side was Kelvar Didatra, a blacksmith, wielding the massive iron hammer that Derek remembered seeing Pippie nearly knock himself out walking with.

The knight stammered for a moment and then spoke, "If... if you peasants attack me I'll have you all strung up."

"And I'm telling you, as an advisor to the king, under section 31 of the Rights of Non-City Dwellers past under the moons of the Lesser Luna Year; 'He or she who is found to be of betrayal of the will of one who is of order to the king, may be exonerated by those of the individuals dwelling in the same settlement as the offender if suitable evidence is not with good standing in the case of the representative of the kingdom. If the representative of the kingdom refuses this then those residing within the settlement affected may take up arms in defiance.' Y'see young man, we know all too well that bad eggs make it under the protection of the kingdom from time to time. And I know a bad egg when I see one, and your Sir Beef Stuck-up-off or whatever his name is, is obviously bloody rotten. And you are the same. So we created laws to protect the honest villager from bullies like you. You may be able to swan around here doing this and that, but if you touch even one hair on that boy's head, then I'll have your head mounted on top of my fireplace before you can cry for your mummy."

The knight stepped away from Derek yet again and began edging away from the angry villagers. Derek had never seen this kind of fire in any of the men here that he'd seen every day for his entire life, and he certainly had no idea that Mr Kelderan was once an advisor to the king! The knight continued to step away and after what looked like a safe distance, he turned away. At that very moment, a monumental, metal to metal clang rang out. The epicentre of which was the helmet of the embarrassed night. Derek turned to see the glistening clean, rock solid ladle that he'd been on the receiving end of so many times, just as it bounced off of the knights head. The ringing seemed to last forever and the thought of how loud it was inside the helmet made Derek shudder. The knight scurried away, trying to take the helmet off. Although the ringing was very loud, he must have heard Derek's mum, still clutching at the ladle, shouting and swearing after him, warning him to stay away.

XIX

One week exactly had now passed since Sir Beef Stroganoff first came to Doko Village and began the lock down. It felt like there was a man in armour with green markings at every crossroad, all with either a smug look or a frown on their face. Even though it was claimed that the lock down was for the safety of the villagers, it felt more like they were there to keep the villagers in a prison. Every villager that walked past was followed and examined like they were criminals. On the East side of the village, where the main entrance from the road was and on towards Bikhin Forest and Dragon's peak, the security was even tighter. Sir Beef had erected himself two fabric tents; one larger one to conduct his research and one smaller one as living quarters. Even the smaller one, Derek noted, was at least twice the size of the average home in Doko Village.

Above the entrance to the living quarters was the Stroganoff coat of arms; a green serpent wrapped around a stone with a yellow lightning bolt. Above the larger tent was the crest of the Zeehan Kingdom; a shield split into four parts with four different ancient runes. The rune symbols are *Kallahalla* meaning Strength, *Vabreega* meaning Loyalty, *Higimm* meaning Integrity, and finally *Dorth* meaning Honour. The four principles that any member of the Zeehan

Kingdom knows well, passed down for generation from the old language of the region to the new.

The main tent had two guards outside of it each in metal armour with green markings and wielding a halberd (a halberd is a long pole weapon with a spear tip and an axe head). The guards stand both sides of the tent entrance with their weapon to their right, blunt end on the ground, and relatively unmoving. Derek noticed that even when people went in and out they didn't seem to even look at them; he wasn't sure how they knew who the person going in was.

Day eight, Derek noted, since the lock down. The light of the sun cast a shadow of Dragon's Peak across the land, blocking the direct sunlight in the early morning. The rain had continued on and off since the other morning and Derek was again watching over the village he called home from atop the roof of his mud hut. There was smoke wafting its way up into the sky from the direction of Sir Beef's new tents he had setup, apparently Derek was no longer the earliest riser in Doko Village. Pippie had promised to be up and ready on time today (Derek left him behind before for his morning practice because he was slow to get up) but today he decided he'd enjoy the company and climbed down from his roof and set off for Pippie's home. Derek remembered what happened when he slipped and decided it'd probably be best not to be seen by any of Sir Beef's armour-clad men. Thankfully, the armour made them easy to see and hear coming, even in the low light of a rainy morning.

He checked his right and left corners coming out from the stacked boxes to see a clear path in the shadows up to the wall of Mr Kelderan's home. Keeping himself low, he made his way across to the wall and knelt down behind a table leg watching the wider walkway that led towards the West of the village and deeper into the heartland of Sir Beef's occupied forces. Derek edged forward ever so slightly while remaining under the table to see around the corner to the left. He edged forward another inch and strained his neck to peek. He looked back behind him, clear, in front, clear, and then again to the right… NOT CLEAR! The soft mud has muffled the clutter and clamour of the armour worn by Sir Beef's troops. The soft step surprised him but he instinctively pulled back.

Derek stayed crouched and held his breath, eyes wide open, hoping that he hadn't been seen. Mr Kelderan had stood up for Derek before but maybe if he was caught under his table, he wouldn't be so lucky. The metal feet stepped and stomped right, left, and right, left, up to the table… then past the table. Derek sighed… but too soon! The legs then turned and walked the outside of the table. The metal legs continued to march right, left, right, left, Derek curled himself a little tighter under the table, breath held, he looked to the ground hoping that the owner of the feet wouldn't feel they were being watched to somehow make himself even less likely to be caught.

The metal feet continued to walk right, left, right, left, past the table and continued down the path.

The adrenaline surged in Derek's body making his legs burn and his hands shake. He remembered to breathe and slowly started in and out. He looked at the figure that was no longer obscured by being under the table to see one of Sir Beef's men walking down the path with his head up high and glancing around, half asleep. 'Lucky he was so snobby,' Derek thought, 'wouldn't see a horse in front of him, his nose is so turned up.'

Derek collected himself and again looked out from under Kelderan's table which had just doubled up as the Kingdom's greatest Turnip Knight in training's hiding spot. The path was clear. Staying low, he continued to hug the wall of Kelderan's house and around to the left to follow the road to Pippie's home. He passed under a window and kept his eyes sharp looking out for every hiding place and shadowy spot he could find. 'Hopefully all of the troops on duty this morning are as snobby as the last one,' Derek thought to himself. He continued another fifty metres or so, past a few more homes and to another major crossroad. As he got closer he could faintly hear the murmur of voices. They became clearer and clearer the closer he got.

The final hut before the opening to the crossroads and Derek found a table and chair to perch near and look around the corner to see the source of the voices without being completely exposed. Every minute he spent was another minute that the sun would rise and illuminate the village, making Derek all the more visible. He didn't recognise the voices, and considering Derek knew most of the people in Doko Village he knew what to expect. He peered around the corner to see two troops in armour with green marking stood outside by the next major crossroad that Derek had to cross to get to Pippie's house. For so early in the morning they were extremely loud and not very considerate to people trying to sleep. They stood facing each other less than two metres away from the corner where Derek was in hiding. Derek had to stop for a moment and consider his options; he could try and distract them or he could possibly go wider around but that would mean potentially running into more troops, plus it would take longer and the sun is coming up. Derek could hear them now.

"So I said to this girl 'oi, why don't you come get yourself a real man, eh?' and I looked at her bloke who was there."

"Oh yeah, what he say?"

"Nothing, mate, nothing, just glared at me hunched over on the seat."

"Ha! Bloody coward mate."

"Yeah so then the guy that owns the pub comes over and starts giving me lip saying I'm trying to start something, right."

"Oh yeah."

"Yeah, yeah, so I looks at him and I flash my crest and I'm like, c'mon then, what you gonna do? Hahaha."

"Bet he ran off then, didn't he."

"Well nah he was like 'yeah nah I don't care about none of that, just don't go intimidatin' my punters'."

"Phwoar, bet you didn't stand for that."

"Nah mate, I stepped up, yeah, and I was like 'chill out mate, I'm just trying to do the lady a favour' and he's looking at me like, you know how they look at ya' when they're trying to be tough but actually proper scared."

"Yeah, yeah, I know, I know."

"So anyway I was like 'tell you what darling, I'll be off now, you want a real man you can follow me' haha!"

"And did she?"

"… Well no… As it happens, while I was walking down the stairs to leave, I tripped up and fell to the bottom of the staircase and the punters laughed at me. Had to get my mum to clean up a cut I got on my elbow."

"Oh…"

"Yeah not the best. Anyway, wanna' head back? Nought going on here, these locals ain't up to much."

The guards walked on by Derek, lingering in the shadows. They didn't notice him as they were too busy chatting away to each other about nothing important. Derek was sure they were gone before progressing onwards. He darted across the opening and into the safety of the clutter of the next homes along. Not long now until he reaches Pippie's place.

XX

The sun has continued to rise while Derek waited for the guards to move on. It was still early enough for guards to be suspicious of a young Turnip Knight in training but now it was also light enough that he was easily visible, even the shadows were getting more conspicuous. Another 100 metres of shifting left and right under cover and he made it to Pippie's place.

Derek knew from being inside, exactly the layout of Pippie's home and where his bedroom was. He edged along the wall and around to the left towards the second window. His hands on the window sill, on the tippiest most tips of his toes, Derek could just about see over the top and into the window. He lifted his head more to glance in, looking down his nose he could just about see into Pippie's bedroom. On the left was a desk with various newspapers and notepads, next to which was Pippie's wardrobe. Derek lost some strength in his legs from straining and had to lift himself up again. He panned around the room further to the right where he now spotted the door to the bedroom and – WHACK –the window opened, right into Derek's face. He was knocked backwards off his feet and onto the ground. The window had clipped his nose and his head right between the eyes, and then continued to his helmet. The force of the hit to the helmet knocked it clean off. Pain throbbed through Derek's head and the quick drop to the ground left him wondering which way was left, right, or even up. He clutched his face and sucked in through his teeth while rocking side to side on the wet muddy ground hoping the pain would go.

Pippie, Derek's oldest and best friend, hadn't noticed Derek at all. Not when he went to open his window, not when he hit Derek while opening the window and not while he stuck his head out and had a stretch to welcome in some fresh air to start his day. He yawned briefly and slowly opened his eyes eventually looking down and seeing his oldest and best friend Derek lying on the floor, clutching at his face and rolling around in the mud sucking his teeth and moaning.

*

"You know you could have just knocked on the front door, my mum's been up for a while, she could have let you in."

"I was just checking if you were in there and I was about to knock on your window."

"Where else would I be?"

"Well I don't know; you could have been coming to wake me up like you did the other week!"

"Shhhhhh, shut up, my mum doesn't know about that. Anyway, it's basically morning, not the dead of night."

"Yeah but these guards hate me. I told you about what happened with Mr Kelderan, remember?"

"So you snuck all the way here? How many guards were there?"

"I dunno, like fifty."

"Fifty, you snuck past fifty guards on a route that has maybe thirty homes? The village must be swarming with them!"

"Well… I don't know I wasn't counting. It felt like fifty."

"And what's your plan now? Have you seen Neek at all?"

"No, I haven't seen him. Do you think he knows about the big tents Beef has set up? They must be getting ready to find the dragon soon. What if Neek is right about Beef?"

"Maybe we should tell Neek about it, then."

"The main gate is blocked by Beef!"

"Then we'll go around."

Pippie, Derek realised, was very good at lying. He was so good at it, he almost had Derek fooled as well. There he was telling his mum how he was going to be going to play at different places around the village at different times and he'd eat at a specific time and a specific place and then he'd be sat in a tree he liked to sit in and read… he was fluent and totally convincing. And his mother absolutely bought it.

"Wow Pip, you're so good at lying!"
"You just have to play it cool and almost start believing it yourself."

The boys set off towards the edge of the village. It was later in the morning now so more people were awake and moving around. Even so, Derek assured Pippie it was better not to be seen as much as possible and although Derek agreed that being inconspicuous was key, he still refused to leave behind his wooden justice sword. Derek compromised and left behind his helmet; today at least the helmet proved to be more of a hindrance; "and it also got in the way during the battle with the goblin," Pippie patronisingly reminded him.

Sword in holster for Derek and notepad in hand for Pippie (in case they needed to take notes) the two boys set off for the edge of the village off the usual path and out towards Bikhin Forest to look for Neek. Since they'd last seen Neek, the village had gained far too many troops of Sir Beef's regiment for Derek's liking, as well as the tents setup at the main village entrance. The boys stayed away from the main roads on their way towards the edge of Doko Village, passing between tight gaps and villagers going about their early morning business. They neared the end of the first step of their journey and stopped just outside of the home of Lilliana and Rusty Gheria.

Lilliana and Rusty had recently moved out to Doko Village from further North. Derek had seen them a few times but didn't really know them that well. Their home sits right on the edge of the Village, meaning it has a little bit of garden both in front and behind it. Lilliana seemed to spend a lot of her time tending to the carrot patch they had in the front garden. There was a wooden bucket left outside, just next to where Derek and Pippie was crouching, inside were carrots of all different colours; orange, yellow, white and purple, but all slightly muddy and with long green ends still attached. The boys were careful not to destroy any of the crops on their approach to the house, they moved the bucket out of the way and Derek crouched down with the weight of his friend Pippie on his shoulders as he leaned over him to also look. Just down from where the main road in and out of the village connected to the main road connecting the village to the city of Zeehan, stood the two tents set up by Sir Beef and his troops.

XXI

The makeshift base was bustling and crowded. Many troops wearing armour of different amounts walked back and forth, left to right and chatting in groups. Some of the troops had a full set of heavy armour while others had light trousers and a small breastplate made of leather. Some had large swords and others had bow and arrows. But all, Pippie pointed out to Derek, had green markings and bore the insignia of Sir Beef Stroganoff. A simplified version of the full coat of arms atop his personal tent; each soldier had on them a serpent with green markings and a lightning bolt.

The boys counted roughly twenty men in all which sunk Derek's claim that he got past around fifty of them on the way to Pippie's house. Pippie got out his notepad and began to scribble. He wrote down; approximate numbers of troops, types of weapons, types of armour/clothing being worn and then also drew a quick rough map of the layout. He jotted down the tents, the benches in front that sat troops and the fire pit to the right of that where last night's fire was dying down.

"We need to find a way through without being seen." Derek told Pippie, ready to move.

"Hold on, just let me take some notes down and we'll have a look at what's going on here for a bit first."

"C'mon Pip, we don't have time, Beef might have already left to go to Dragon's Peak."

"I don't think so. Wouldn't they all be there doing that? It looks like they're still preparing."

"So we still have time, c'mon let's go!"

"We don't even know where Neek is, he may have gone already. Also Derek, it might help if we have something to actually show Neek rather than just finding him for no reason."

At that moment, the opening to the tent was pulled aside and out walked Sir Beef Stroganoff. Just as he was in the village when Derek first saw him, Sir Beef walked with his head held high up into the clouds and with his chin leading. Sir Beef was not a particularly large man, and seemed to scurry along with lots of little steps and no movement of his upper body. He walked himself out from the shadows from inside the tent and another figure followed him.

A short stature, with armour like nothing Derek had ever seen before and possibly the only person there with no green markings or serpent on them whatsoever. Out of the shadows and into the muggy light of day, the figure came into better focus; armoured from head to toe, but the armour seemed lightweight and effortless for the figure to move in. The boots had three points like eagle talons and blue spikes popped out from the top facing upwards and outwards from the calf. The armour had what looked like a skirt, but it was again blue and pointy. The chest plate shone bright silver with spikes at the shoulder and a blue emblem on the front of a creature with a huge mouth open wide. The helmet was most spectacular of all; it covered all but the face and had what looked like two wings coming out from the top. Derek fixated his eyes on this new figure in awe. Then he noticed the spear; at least as long as the person was tall, it sat across the back at an angle with a golden point at its tip. The bottom was finished with a golden ball.

"Pip, who's that?"

"Woooh, no clue. Looks cool though."

"I wonder where you get a suit like that from."

"There's no green on it and I don't know what the symbol on the front is."

"Never seen a spear like that before, either."

"Same here. This is really bad."

"What? Why?"

"That looks like an extremely powerful warrior, Derek. And that extremely powerful warrior is standing with Sir Beef."

XXII

The boys made their way from the cover of mud and wood huts, boxes and cabbage patches and away from the tents to try and cross the road out of sight and into the shade of Bikhin Forest. They moved up further and further away which took them slightly down hill and giving them more of a chance of staying out of sight. The whole of Doko Village is surrounded by a wall that's just about taller than Derek and Pippie, this made it perfect cover but also extremely hard to see over. They continued their journey and eventually the tents were out of sight over the wall, neither of the boys were sure which garden they were in now and was hoping it was someone either very nice, very old, or very blind.

"We need to get over the wall, Derek."

"Yeah, boost me up."

"Okay I'll try. Watch your head though, one of Beef's goons might take it clean off."

"On second thought, maybe you should be the one to go over. After all, I've been doing all the training I'll be able to lift you up easier."

"Yeah… but… no. You're the big hero of vegetation; you should be brave and go first."

"Well I have a fear of heights!"

"Since when? You stand on the roof of your house every morning!"

"Since I was looking for you and I got taken out by a window! That's when!"

"Shhhhhh, stop shouting. All right we'll think of something."

Pippie looked around. And then he looked further down the wall. "Ah, look! Right there!"

The wall, made of grey pieces of stone, had fallen inwards creating a convenient gap through to the road without having to climb up the entire height of the wall. In the muggy weather the stone was slippery to step on but Derek led the voyage out from the confines of the village and onto the main road. Derek had never been out this far from the entrance to the village or this side of Bikhin Forest because the route to the safe rope bridge is in a slightly different direction. Bikhin Forest is vast and extends much further along the road with Dragon's Peak looming over. But this far along the road has no entry because of the ten foot rocky bank.

"We need to find a way into the forest around this bank. When you go in the forest to practice, what ways do you get in?"

"I get in right next to where those tents are. No chance at the moment. It wasn't a problem before but they don't seem happy to see me anymore."

"Hmmm… was hoping you'd know of another route. Maybe if we go further along we can follow the river back in?"

"Where we want to be is up high though. If we go that way we'll be at the bottom of the waterfall."

"Yeah but you remember we originally saw Neek down there before the battle with the goblin."

"Oh yeah. But my mum always says I shouldn't go down there. Even in the day it's a high risk area for monster attacks. And if I'm being honest, Pip, I don't think my sword is much good."

"And I haven't been able to cast any spells since the goblin battle. Rather not risk it just in case it doesn't work."

"Arrrgggg… this is so annoying. NEEEEEEEKKKKK! WHERE ARE YOU?"

"SHHHHHH… Derek! Shut up, Beef's goons might hear you."

There was rustling from atop the bank that leads into Bikhin Forest. Pippie took a step back, startled. His heart pumped hard in his chest. Could it be another goblin taking a chance in the daylight? Maybe one of Beef's goons? A rusty voice came from the forest-

"Yes?" The face of Neek appeared.

XXIII

Neek, still in his large cloak and hood, appeared from within the thick brush of the forest. Neek took to his knee and held out his arm, pulling the boys up the bank, one at a time. He then signalled them deeper into the forest and the boys followed. The three of them went through the trees, Neek leading the way. After a minute or so, they came to a small opening where Neek had a tent of his own set up.

Unfortunately, the tent wasn't quite as marvellous as the ones that Sir Beef had. It stood no taller than Derek, meaning you'd need to sit down to be in it and probably wouldn't fit more than two fully grown adults at a squeeze. It had no crest above the entrance and seemed to be very simply made; possibly just two or three sticks and whatever basic material Neek had to hand to drape over it. Outside was a small fire burning; a pile of small sticks stacked up with embers glowing in the centre. A few stones, roughly the third of the size of Derek, sat around the fire, clean from the muddy ground. The boys sat down on a rock each, with Neek sitting on the third. He sat with his arms leaning on his knees and hunched forward, he looked at the boys one at a time with a smile.

"Nice place." Derek broke the silence.

"It's just a temporary pop up, standard practice for anyone on the road."

"How did you know we needed you Neek? Derek and I didn't know how to contact you."

"Well I heard Derek shout. I was just there."

"See Pip? Easy solution. You need something you just ask for it."

"You could have alerted Sir Beef, Derek! We got lucky!"

"Oh? You didn't know I was here? I thought I told you I'd be here?"

"Sir, you told us you were staying in the area but not where we can find you."

"Ah, well, sorry about that. Did you say something about Sir Beef? What about him?"

"Show him your drawings, Pip."

Pippie passed over the drawings and notes he created that documented the number of Sir Beef's troops, their weapons, and a layout of his tents. Neek nodded and grunted positively while looking over the information.

"Hmm, yes, I see. This is exactly what I expected to see. Good work boys."

"Thank you, sir. We thought you'd want to know what he's up to."

"What we have here is a full-scale preparation camp setup with his immediate battalion and also, I assume, his ground group."

"What's a ground group?"

"Did you see heavily armoured grunts with green markings and a basic sword walking around irritating the villagers and looking everyone they come across up and down like criminals?"

"Yeah! How did you know?"

"That's his ground group. The ground group are his lowest level fighters. They're the very definition of a 'grunt', just there to earn a basic living and walk around in armour. They have basic weapon's training and basic understanding of the kingdoms laws. No more than anyone else living in Zeehan. Their purpose is to keep you under check. From the perspective of Beef and his base camp, they're just here to cause disruption for the locals to make it easier for him to manoeuvre without the scrutiny of the locals."

"Wow. Sir Beef really is smart."

"He is a strong tactician, Pip."

"Oh yeah Pip, what about that other guy? Tell Neek about the spear."

Pippie described the warrior they saw with the magnificent blue armour and the spear with golden tips. Neek seemed troubled when hearing the description. The colour left his face.

"And you're sure? Boots with claws like talons? Wings on the helmet? A large pole weapon?"

"Yes. Sure."

"How big was this person?"

"Well they were far away but stood next to Sir Beef. I'd say they were about half a foot shorter than Sir Beef." There was a pause.

"I know who it is." Neek sounded very serious.

"Really? Who?"

"Karakawt."

"Cara-what?"

"Karakawt. Karakawt the Dragoon."

"Dragoon?"

"What's a Dragoon?"

"Well boys… as you know there are many people in this world that travel around either as part of missions assigned by their kingdoms or as adventurers. There are other incentives for people to travel around to different regions and battle different monsters along the way. Some people become specialists in fighting certain monsters, and sometimes these specialisations are ancient tradition."

"And this is one of 'those' times, I'm guessing?"

"It is. The ancient art of the Dragoon class of warrior is steeped in tradition. They are trained warriors with specialised armour and weapons, always some form of pole such as a spear, and they are especially skilled at killing dragons."

"So do you think Sir Beef wants the dragon killed?"

"Possibly. There is a chance that he actually doesn't."

"Why would you have a Dragoon around if you don't plan on killing the dragon?"

"This particular Dragoon, Karakawt, is an old friend of mine."

"A friend? Well that's got to be a good thing surely."

"You misunderstand. What I mean is that Karakawt is a rival. *She* is a fighter for hire and one that I have battled with in the past. She and I are matched in strength and a battle between the both of us would be impossible to predict the outcome. Although as it stands, I don't have my master-crafted weapon and that would put me at a disadvantage. Karakawt has extremely well crafted weapons and armour. Karakawt on her own would probably wipe the floor with me, but her teamed up with Beef would be an impossible battle. Beef also has accurate archers and a team of middle-class foot soldiers in his battalion. The odds are certainly stacked against me here."

"Us." Derek had been quiet for a while.

"Excuse me?"

"I think you're forgetting that you aren't on your own, Neek. You got me and Pip here by your side."

"And do you really think you are strong enough to be an effective force in a battle against Beef? I don't mean to offend you boys but you struggled to survive an encounter with a goblin. I admit I see massive potential in you both but you have years of training before you can even match the lowest level fighter that Beef has at his disposal."

"There's more than one way to rid your bed of Killicockers, Neek. I know my wooden sword isn't that strong and Pip can't cast spells but we can still do stuff. We told you about the Dragoon, remember?"

"Derek is right, Neek. Maybe there are other things we can do in the fight. Sir Beef doesn't seem like a decent guy, you do. If you think he's up to something bad then we have to do what we can to stop him."

"No! It's too dangerous! Karakawt will butcher you both without a second thought. Beef will have no prisoners on his mission. He is a Sir of the highest order to the Kingdom of Zeehan; he has full power to do as he wishes to whomever that he may find blocking his way whilst on official business. There's no way you can survive an encounter and I'm not putting you two in danger for the sake of anything. Now go home! Go home and hide yourself and wait for this to pass. In a month you will have forgotten we were even here and will be back to your normal daily life."

"Neek, we—"

"LEAVE!" Neek bellowed loud like his lungs were reinforced with steel, a haze seemed to flow out of him as the raw magical energy flooded out and hit the boys, almost knocking them off of their stones. The fire burnt brighter than ever and then went out almost instantly. Derek and Pippie, shaking, got up and scurried away. They made their way back to the road, got down the bank and hopped through the hole in the city wall.

They said nothing all the way back to the village.

XXIV

It was late morning by the time Derek and Pippie got back into the more populated part of the village. They joined the main walking path and ventured deeper, ignoring the guards and locals on the way. They passed one of the more popular watering wells which is situated near an opening and sat down on the ground together. The two boys have sat there often as there always seems to be a little bit of hay there which makes the ground nice to sit on.

"Neek flipped his lid." Derek said, looking at the ground.

"Must be stressed."

"Yeah but he still went over the top."

"Maybe."

"Huh? Why only 'maybe'? You know he did."

"Well maybe he's right, Derek. Maybe we aren't really cut out for any of this right now."

"What? Pip, you as well?"

"Neek is more powerful than we can comprehend, Derek. And he's scared of this Karakawt the Dragoon."

"Yeah, so?"

"Have you ever even heard of a Dragoon before? They're known to be super powerful, but Neek said this one is extremely powerful. We saw how easily Neek killed that goblin, and for us that goblin was too much. You felt how powerful Neek was when he yelled. We're in over our heads."

"That doesn't mean we can't…"

"… yes Derek. It does mean we can't do anything. I mean you already got lucky with Mr Kelderan getting you out of trouble. If you were strong like Neek or Karakawt are, then you could have taken out that guard and moved on without a problem."

"Pip…"

"But you're not. You're just a little boy with a bit of wood running about hitting a tree. You aren't that brave Derek, you only go out of the village in the day and you stick to the safest route through to the rope bridge. You know even the other kids in our class have climbed the tree across the drop instead of using that rope bridge."

"I was going to one day I'm just getting going."

"No Derek, you're just not a hero. Stop making excuses for yourself and get over it."

"…"

"Neek is right, we're being stupid we should just lay low and wait for it all to blow over."

"… stupid…"

"I'm going home. Goodbye Derek, I'll see you when school starts up again."

Derek sat for a while, alone. People around him bustled left and right but Derek sat still on the comfy ground a little while longer.

The walk home seemed to take hours for Derek. He strolled slowly along the path staring at the ground. The people around him became like a mist in his vision. He didn't stop to get scraps of food from anyone; he didn't look up to glare at any of Sir Beef's men. He just kept walking home. He turned the last corner to see his mum sat outside with a sandwich and talking to Mr Kelderan.

"Oh, hello Delly. Didn't expect you back at this time."

"…"

Derek went indoors and into his room. Pippie, his best friend in the entire world, had let him down. Pippie has never had a bad word to say about Derek for as long as they've known each other and even though he didn't believe in the myth of the Turnip Knight he never mocked Derek for it. Not like the other children at school. Derek removed his wooden justice sword and holster made out of rabbit skin and placed it on the ground.

Derek stared at the wall.

XXV

Night descended. Day ascended. For the first time in over a year Derek was woken by the light of the sun coming into his bedroom. Derek got up, got dressed, and left his bedroom. But he was surprised to see his mother waiting for him on the other side looking concerned.

"Delly. Are you okay?"

"I don't like it when you call me that, Mum."

"Why haven't you already gotten up and gone out? Are you feeling sick?"

"No."

"Did a guard tell you off again? You know they can't stop you walking around here."

"Yes I know."

"Then what's wrong?"

"…"

"Derek?"

"Can I go outside to eat my breakfast?"

"Okay."

Derek sat outside with his breakfast (leftover rabbit stew and bread) with his head down. He focussed entirely on the food when he heard the familiar old voice of Mr Kelderan.

"No beasts for you to slay today, little Turnip Knight?"

"No such thing as a Turnip Knight."

"Hahahahaha! Says who? You claimed to be a Turnip Knight and now you say they don't exist? Then do you not exist?"

"…"

"What's gotten you down, young man?"

"Mr Kelderan, you know my dad. Is he brave?"

"Brave? Well my boy, he's either incredibly brave or awfully stupid. There isn't a huge difference in the two to begin with."

"So how can I be brave rather than stupid?"

"In order for someone to be brave rather than stupid, the thing that they do must work out in their favour."

"I don't get it."

"Well, let's take you and your little friend for example, sneaking out the other week."

"Shhhhh, Mr Kelderan, how'd you know about that?" Derek brought the conversation to a whisper, Mr Kelderan obliged.

"Not important. What is important is that you did something that was remarkably stupid. You are a young boy with no real combat training, going unarmed into a thick wood in an area that is teeming with nastiness, just like the goblin you encountered."

"How do you know about that?"

"Now, if you had died, then that would have been awfully stupid of you and all the villagers here that would have buried you would have said you were very stupid and it's no wonder you died. Do you understand?"

"Yeah, but I didn't die. Pip and I got through it."

"You and Pip were fortunate that Neek was there. But regardless, you went into danger in search of answers and you lived to tell the tale. Therefore, you were quite brave to do so."

"But it was Pip who suggested we go. Maybe it's Pip that's brave and not me."

"On the contrary, your little friend would not have gone without you. He is not so stupid or so brave to venture out there without you. Maybe he sees something in you that you do not."

"Yeah, well, he don't see that in me no more."

"Oh Derek, you silly, brave little boy. You are only just beginning your journey in this world and you must now understand that the future is fraught with adversary and negativity. Your ability to stand against that is what makes you a hero."

"But what about when your friends don't believe in you?"

"Give them something to believe in."

"Mr Kelderan, how do you know so much about me?"

"Well for starters, you wake me up in the morning with your damn climbing! You aren't very agile, Derek. The other morning, you certainly would have been seen by the guard if I hadn't blown some Cerantarian mist out the window."

"Ceran-what?"

"The Cerantarian plant creates an aroma that can un-sharpen the senses. I just blew a little at the guard as he walked by and he was away with the fairies."

"What about the other guards?"

"I didn't help you with any other guards, so if you managed to avoid them, then that was on you. Well done, young Turnip Knight."

"Okay but then how did you know about the goblin?"

"I used to work for the Zeehan Court, boy. Neek is an old friend."

"So you've been sneaking out of the village to update Neek as well?"

"No I've been using other means to contact him. Although it is very basic and designed to send military information such as numbers and positioning. We can't have in-depth conversations like you would face to face and that's where I was hoping you'd help me out."

Derek explained to Kelderan what had happened when he and Pippie met up with Neek last.

"Bah! The silly old fool! You know, for such a smart man, he really is dumb! First sign of things not going his way; he always lashes out at those closest to him. Right, I need to have a think…"

"Should I come back in a few…"

"-This is what we'll do!"

"Wow Mr Kelderan you think fast."

"Listen, this Dragoon is a bit of a bump in the road, but not the end of the line, if you get what I mean."

"Not really, no."

"Direct combat is a definitive no-go. That's probably what has Neek uptight. He loves a good scrap."

"You're speaking a bit fast right now."

"We can pre-occupy the Dragoon if we create the right legal distraction."

"You're pacing a bit fast; you're making a hole in the mud."

"According to Warrior Code, Section 13: legal combative action close to civilisation, there must be a full report created by the party to prove minimal damage to the village."

"I'm so lost right now."

"Paragraph 3 states very clearly: 'Any resident may demand to see the report and have a copy made, in full, and presented in no less than 24 hours, during which time no further action can be taken.' Derek! That's it!"

"I don't know what you're talking about."

"We can stall them with a W.C. Section 13 Surroundings Report request."

"So we stall them, then what?"

"Well then while that's being done, Neek can get up that mountain, the rest is between Neek and I."

"So you and Neek have a plan? That's great."

"Yes but I need you to help with it."

"How?"

"You know where Neek is camping, you can deliver the message. I told you our communication is simple, I can't convey that much information to him and I'm a bit too old to be sneaking around trying to find him."

"So you want me to go?"

"My boy, I wouldn't usually ask you or any young person to put themselves at risk, but as it stands, you know how to get to Neek and you're small enough to not be seen. These are strange times for our village and that causes for strange solutions."

"Are you calling me strange?"

"No! You silly boy... Oh it doesn't matter. Let's focus on what's important here; I need you to tell Neek everything I've just told you."

"You must be joking."

"Ah, yes, not well versed in law. Well then I need to send Neek a note but I'm worried that if you're caught we'll be done. It is imperative that you aren't caught, Derek."

"I'll do my best."

Kelderan disappeared for ten minutes and came back with a note and a small gold coin. He instructed Derek to give Neek the note along with the coin. "The coin is a symbol of trust for members of Zeehan. Neither of us is part of that any more but Neek will understand that by giving you this coin, I put my trust in you, Derek. But for god's sake boy, don't get caught or they'll have everything."

XXVI

Derek set off without delay to get to Neek and his temporary camp. Kelderan said he would use his basic messaging system to contact Neek to "instruct him to hold fast" in position. It was down to Derek now to get to Neek and deliver the message. That's it. That would be Derek's role in all this...

Early afternoon meant that the guards were lax with people moving around in the village; that was good for Derek, who decided it was probably best for him during this mission to leave his Turnip Knight equipment at home in order to blend in better with the rest of the civilians. Getting to the collapsed part of the wall would be the easy part but once outside of the wall, Derek could be in real danger if one of Beef's men spots him.

He quickly made his way to the outskirts of the village towards the part of the city wall that Pippie and he last used to get out from the village and towards Neek's temporary camp. Derek had spent so much time in the forest; he knew it very well by this point and was sure he could get to Neek's camp with relative ease.

Derek arrived quickly outside the front of the house that stood between him and his exit from Doko Village. He looked left and right checking for guards and other villagers, now was the time where he would look out of place and not just another villager passing through.

Derek stopped and loitered for a moment, shifting his weight left and right and looking at the ground. 'You're just a kid hanging around not up to much,' Derek thought to himself, trying to get into the character of someone not worth looking at. Unfortunately for Derek, he had built up quite the reputation in the village for his early morning training and he was getting far too many hellos for his liking.

After a few minutes, Derek slowly started to shuffle awkwardly towards the front of the house. He took what felt like the only opportunity and dashed between the fence and around the side of the house. This was a lot harder than he thought it would be. If only Pippie was here to help him…

No! Pippie had let him down and now he had to do this himself.

Derek continued around the side of the home towards the back, he turned the corner to find freshly laid wall in the exact place where the hole used to be! "Crap," Derek muttered to himself. "How am I gonna get over this now?" He persisted and decided to have a look anyway. The wall was indeed rebuilt; the rocks stacked up again and the mud holding it together darker than the rest of the wall. It was obviously made recently. Derek tried to boost himself up over the top but it was too high. If only Pippie was here to give him a boost…

Derek tried to climb up again… and fell. He tried again… and he fell again. One more time… this time he got his footing for a moment and then thudded back to the ground. Derek sat still, wondering what he could do. 'Just can't get over this wall,' he thought to himself. Maybe Pippie was right after all.

Derek is no hero, really. He's just some kid in a village playing around with a bit of wood and waking up early. He isn't skilled, he's not strong, he can't fight… he won't even cross the waterfall using the tree instead of the safe rope bridge. Derek started to really accept that he was useless.

He sat there on the ground, staring at the wall. What more can he do? He has a note and a coin and he can't get them to Neek. He had failed. Kelderan said that he trusted him with this task and he failed it. Derek fidgeted with the wall, picking away at the mud. It was still quite soft and easy to move between the rocks. Before long, he could fit a few fingers in the hole quite deeply. He got up and made more of these holes in the wall all the way up.

Before too long, the wall had handle holes all the way to the top. Derek put his foot in the lowest one and tested it. It took his weight without a problem. Once again, he scaled the wall using the handle holes he'd created to help him and easily reached the top. The coast was clear on the other side, so he quickly flicked over the top and dropped to the bottom. Before giving it a single thought, he ran fast at the bank that led up to Bikhin Forest and managed to run up just high enough to latch on to a branch sticking out. Derek then pulled himself up and into the shadow of the forest.

He began his journey into the forest.

XXVII

Derek hadn't thought about it until now, but he really did know the forest well. He wasn't sure exactly how he knew it so well (he didn't really recognise specific trees or anything like that) but he just knew exactly where to go.

He walked between the trees that shadowed him from the sky, turning left and turning right being sure not to trip on any exposed roots or step in any soft mud and ruin his shoes. Before long he came across the opening in the forest where Neek had set up camp. Everything was as it was before; the small tent and the fire pit with stones around it. But no Neek.

Derek moved quickly and with urgency and stepped up to the tent and knocked on the single stick holding the front of the tent up. "Neek?" He loudly whispered, aware that patrols may have spread now into the forest. He knocked again and called out again, but this time he knocked too hard and the tent collapsed! The fabric fell and the second stick holding the back of the tent up fell into to what was left of Neek's living quarters. 'Hope he isn't an afternoon napper,' Derek thought to himself.

Derek scrabbled at first to try and pick the sticks back up but it was no use. Derek looked around to see no one in sight... Kelderan was meant to get a message out to Neek to stay at his base, so where is he? Maybe he didn't get the message yet?

"You shouldn't have come back, Derek."

Derek turned to see the familiar rugged face of Neek staring back at him. For such a large figure he seemed very illusive and managed to creep his way up to Derek very easily.

"How are you so quiet?"

"Why are you here?"

"I asked first."

"You're very cocky for a boy that just broke the home of one of the strongest fighters in the Kingdom."

"Well maybe you should have spent more time learning how to make a sturdy tent, Mr Big Man."

"Why are you here, Derek? I told you to stay away."

"I told you I can help, so I'm helping."

"You broke my tent, you're a hindrance."

"Well I have it on good authority, you're 'dumb'! What do you say to that?"

"I say tread lightly. I don't need a sword to have your head off your shoulders, a stick will do. And if you look around you'll see there are an awful lot of sticks to choose from."

"Well you'll definitely need to show me how to do that. But look what I got." Derek presented Neek with the coin he was given by Kelderan.

"You're working with the Kingdom now? Have you sided with Beef?"

"Not Beef, Old Man Kelderan."

"Kelderan?"

"He's my neighbour, remember? We had a little talk earlier and he asked me to give you this message." Derek handed the note to Neek. "See, I told you I can help."

Neek put up his finger to silence Derek while he read. "The first line of the message says that I am dumb."

"Told you."

"Damn that man. Okay… hmm… I see Section 13… well this is certainly something… yes it is similar to a situation a few years back. I'm still not sure… well yes that is a good point… hmm."

Neek continued to mutter to himself as he passed left and right reading the note from Kelderan. Although Derek didn't really get what was being told to him earlier by Kelderan, he assumed that all the information was there on the note. But this time the person on the receiving end of the information actually understood what was happening.

"Derek, I think this may work."

"I hope so. I still don't quite understand what it's about but I was hoping you would."

"Yes! Yes this can work. I've made contact with a local blacksmith and they're currently crafting me a new weapon. It isn't master crafted level but it'll work for what I need it to do."

"You can get up Dragon's Peak?"

"Yes. And I can get rid of the creature."

"Do what now?"

"Get rid of the dragon."

"I thought you wanted to protect it."

"Well I would if I could, but my goal is to stop Beef from controlling it. I suspect that the previous controller of that dragon is no longer with it and now it sits alone. If the dragon can be controlled then I need to kill it to stop Beef from controlling it."

"Right… well, then, good luck mate. I guess I'll be off home, then."

"Yes! Well done, young Turnip Knight, no need to go and speak to Kelderan, he has already mobilised so you just need to go and be safe."

"So just to make sure I understand everything; you're off now to go up Dragon's Peak?"

"No, not now, but I'll be going when the sun falls behind the horizon."

"So… tonight?"

"Yes."

"Okay. Bye then."

Derek sprinted off back towards the road, he faintly heard Neek say something about meeting up afterward to celebrate but he wasn't interested. Neek planned to kill the dragon? Derek wasn't really sure what he expected but that wasn't what he wanted. Dragons are a rarity and it didn't feel right at all to just go and kill it for no reason.

Maybe he'd been on the wrong side this whole time. Then again, Sir Beef didn't seem like a decent person, either.

Derek decided to create a third side.

XXVIII

Derek sprinted to the edge of the forest. He jumped down the bank that was easily taller than he was. He landed gracefully and darted across the road and vaulted with ease over the wall. Back into the village, he ran as fast as he could, weaving in and out between people, darting left and right. He continued across the main walkway and up towards the roads leading off to the top end of the village.

Finally, he reached Pippie's house.

Derek banged on the door, it was coming towards the early evening now and different food was wafting through the air. Pippie's mother answered the door, a kind and gentle lady who was always very nice to Derek; Derek barged through without a word. He saw Pippie there, grabbed him by the wrist and marched him into his bedroom and shut the door quickly.

Derek explained everything to Pippie. He told him how he had helped Kelderan with delivering a message to Neek who was now preparing to get up to the top of Dragon's Peak and kill the dragon. He wasn't able to explain exactly how Kelderan would distract Beef and the rest of them, but he was able to tell Pippie that it had something to do with some laws. Pippie probably would know more about it than Derek if he was there to have heard it from Kelderan.

"Pip, mate, we got to do something."

"Do what?"

"I dunno, not let anyone get to that dragon."

"How are you going to do that Derek? Got that wooden sword of yours handy?"

"Funny you should say that; Neek said he could take my head off with a stick."

"Yes, *your* head, Derek, because you're powerless against him. And what about Beef and his men? Or the Dragoon? You suddenly able to fight off twenty or so armed fighters, a Zeehan Sir, a former Zeehan Sir *and* a top level Dragoon?"

"Well obviously not, but…"

"… but what? What you planning to do?"

"Mate! Look Pip, I don't know exactly what I'm going to do, and I know I'm not able to fight anyone. I wouldn't be surprised if you could take me on. Actually, you nearly took my head off not long ago with that window. I'm an idiot, but I'm a better idiot when I got you by my side. You dragged me into the woods and nearly got us killed by a goblin. You were there when we first saw Beef in the village and you threw a rock at him. You distracted him so I could fill his horse's pack with poop. You've had my back for ages, mate, and I'm here to tell you that I got to get up that mountain before Beef, or Neek, or that Dragoon does. Now you can either help me or not. But I'm going. I'm going to head home quickly to see if Kelderan is there, then I'm going up Dragon's Peak. If I die, then we'll all remember how stupid I was. If not, then I think we'll all find I've done the right thing."

"…"

"Are you in? C'mon Pip, let's finish this adventure!"

"Goodbye, Derek."

"You know where to find me if you change your mind. I might need that magic spell again."

Derek left without a word to Pippie's mother and headed home.

He felt different. He was most likely about to be completely annihilated by a dragon, Sir Beef, Neek, or Karakawt, the Dragoon. And if not, then his mother surely would when she found out what happened. But even so, he felt lighter, like a weight was lifted, like he could see the world a lot clearer now than he ever could. 'Maybe,' Derek thought, 'maybe I've levelled up a bit.'

The village was looking less busy as most people were now home and eating. A lot of different dishes of food touched at Derek's nose as he passed different windows. All familiar in some way as he'd passed them so many times before. He took the quickest route back home, similar to the route taken the other day but without the need to avoid the men in armour with green markings. He saw Kelderan's house. Kelderan's house had a doorway that faced his own house, meaning in order to knock, Derek risked being in view for his mum to see him and then he'd have to stay and eat and that would slow him down. However, if he was being honest with himself he was very hungry now.

As he approached, he peaked over the bottom of the window into Kelderan's house to see if he was in, no sign of him at all. He continued around the corner and could hear talking... sounded like his mother. His mother's voice and... Kelderan's! Derek turned the corner to see his mother and Kelderan chatting. Talking about the best way to get flavour out of onion when complimenting meat.

"Oh, hello Delly. You okay? You look like you've been sweating. Did you run here?"

"Mum… hey… erm… what we eating?"

"One of your favourite's tonight darling; you've got butternut squash with carrots and sweet potato."

"Cool, I'll just go change out of my sweaty clothes then."

As Derek walked into the house, he turned to catch Kelderan's eyes, just in time for a sly little smirk and a wink. From inside, Derek could hear Kelderan talking to his mother still for a while longer, and then heard him say he had a little errand to run in an hour. Derek had time to really prepare.

He tried to be as normal as possible with his mother at dinner. He made up a story about some adventure he went on with Pippie where they pretended the well was a summoning altar and they were trying to stop an evil wizard from summoning a Demonic Crux Hag. Derek really surprised himself. If Pippie could hear his lying skills, he'd be really proud. All the while, Derek kept one eye on the window, watching for Kelderan to leave.

Derek had no real idea what an hour was. He never was great with time. All he knew was that Kelderan was due to leave in an hour from when he spoke to Derek's mother. Kelderan was definitely the type of person to be exact with his timing. So Derek sat and ate and drank and waited and watched. He finished his meal and still Kelderan hadn't moved. Derek went to his room, turned his lights off and watched outside for some movement from Kelderan.

All night he waited. Finally, before sunrise, he saw Kelderan, in a cloak, leave his house.

XXIX

Kelderan pulled a long, draping hood over his head, covering his face. He checked that he'd properly locked his door (very responsible) and checked left and right before setting off towards the camp set up by Sir Beef and his men. Derek watched, in the darkness of his room, partially covering his face, and peeking out from the corner of his window, until Kelderan was out of sight.

Derek leaned out of his window carefully, checking if the coast was clear for him and waiting until Kelderan's steps had disappeared into the distance before jumping out of his bedroom window and landing gracefully on the muddy ground. Sword in holder, helmet on head, Derek, the Turnip Knight in training, was ready to set off on his next adventure. 'Goodbye, Mum,' he thought to himself, 'I'm off to save a dragon.'

He headed off in the same direction as Kelderan. Sir Beef's makeshift camp was at the edge of the village near Bikhin Forest. Getting through Bikhin Forest would eventually lead to Dragon's Peak. Derek had gone a little further along only once, and that was when he wasn't concentrating one day and missed the turn towards the safe rope bridge. The path was a lot more treacherous than what he was used to but it was the only route he knew.

Derek noticed something; there was a lack of men in armour with green markings about. In fact, there were none at all. For a while now, having a solider clit-clotting around was starting to feel quite normal. Suddenly, the village felt quieter. Silent. Where were they?

One more turning and Derek will have made it to the makeshift camp. He decided to approach this last turning with caution. He got to the edge of the last building between him and the makeshift camp. First Derek leant forward, ear-first to see what he could hear. It was quite far away so could only faintly hear the sound of people's voices. He turned his head and eased forward out of cover until one eye was exposed. He saw exactly what he expected to see; Kelderan was there, hood down, chatting to four guards. One seemed to be engaged in the conversation whereas the other three looked lost and confused. Their main input to the conversation seemed to be the occasional catching of each other's eyes and the odd head scratch.

Derek scoured the area. Learning from his last stake-out of the area with Pippie… wait, Pippie… 'I suppose he really didn't want to come after all,' Derek thought to himself. He looked around and took in the surroundings; multiple groups of combatants with variations of weapons and armour grouped together. Some sat on the benches while others stood around the fire. Derek wanted to count but it was no use; it looked like every soldier that was usually in the village, patrolling, was here, as well as the usual group of combatants and guards that were already here.

Derek looked around more to see if he could spot anyone he knew other than Kelderan; all of these guards all looked the same. All with the same arrogant, smug grin or annoyed frown. Sir Beef couldn't be seen and neither could the Dragoon, Karakawt. It was time to move, somehow past the crowd and into the forest.

Derek moved around to the side and towards the gardens of the homes on the edge of the village. He noticed that although there were more people here now, they all seemed to be focussing in on the camp and not really patrolling the immediate area. Someone small like him could probably get around the absolute edge of the village wall opening, unnoticed. Add to that it was still dark and the light of the fire wasn't carrying very far.

Derek continued forward, pressed against the wall of whatever house was closest. He kept low and kept his eyes panning the area for anyone that could coincidentally look his way and foil him. Derek continued to creep. He crept low and slow. Staying low and staying slow, he inched his way around the edge of the village wall's opening and stayed in the shadows. He stopped to watch again. From this angle, he could see deeper into the crowd, still no Beef. He did however, see an annoyed Kelderan, being dragged by the arm through the crowd and towards the tent belonging to Sir Beef. From where Derek was, it wasn't clear if Kelderan was about to successfully slow down Sir Beef or if they'd chosen not to listen to him and keep him prisoner instead. Either way, it was time to keep moving on.

Derek darted into Bikhin Forest.

XXX

Derek knew that he was at least ahead of Sir Beef's men. If Kelderan was successful, then he'd only need to beat Neek to Dragon's Peak. Where Neek was, exactly, was anyone's guess.

Derek danced across the forest floor he'd grown to know so well. He felt the crunching of twigs and could hear the squashing of dead leaves under his feet; a quick hop to avoid a patch of wet mud here and a step to the side to avoid the large tree roots there. Derek continued his speedy ballet dance through the forest and towards the target. After a few minutes, he came across the road split. One was well trodden on and led to the safe rope bridge, the other was quite overgrown and wild and led towards the dangerous bottom of Dragon's Peak. Derek didn't hesitate. He darted into the overgrown path and ventured on.

The brush here was much thicker. Thick vines had been able to grow and invade with little opposition, giving a dangerous sharp graze to anyone not paying attention for a moment and veering off the narrow pathway. There were occasional pretty flowers on the path, but mostly just dense brush, thick spiky thorns and intimidating trees looming overheard. Visibility was getting slightly easier by the minute as the sun rose, and with the gain of the sun came the loss of chance that a monster might be looking to snatch up an easy target like Derek.

Over a fallen tree and under another, Derek continued on through the forest. It felt like a long time since he'd first ventured into the forest and was sure that he would eventually be out of the woods and into the opening at the bottom of Dragon's Peak. Derek pushed some overbearing branches away from his face as he pressed on, always checking around and keeping his ears open, listening out for anything from Neek or Sir Beef, right through to a Goblin or some other deadly beast.

A few minutes passed and the day continued to slowly shine in. Through the dense trees, Derek could now see a small light. It seemed to glow blue and be floating off the ground. It was also roughly in the direction the path was taking him. He knew it could be any number of things but had to continue. Closer and closer, the small glow seemed to grow and become clearer. By Derek's estimation, he was no more than 100 metres from it now so decided to venture with caution. Back to low and slow.

70 metres now. 50. 30. 20. The edge of the forest. The light was definitely in the opening that was the bottom of Dragon's Peak. Derek stepped off the path and moved behind a tree. He looked out from behind it to see what the glow was. The light could clearly be seen now; a lamp hanging on a stick, stuck in the ground and sturdy. To the right was the familiar small tent that belonged to Neek. It wasn't clear if Neek was home or not. Was Derek too late? Had Kelderan successfully slowed down Sir Beef enough and Neek was already up there? Surely not, it's too dark! Or maybe it's not

too dark for Neek, maybe he's strong enough to venture out in the wild any time.

"I can't be hasty," Derek reasoned to himself. "If Neek is already making his way up the hill, then I have to follow, but if he hasn't and he's here, then maybe I've got more time." Derek stayed and continued to look on, hoping to see or hear some form of movement from the tent. Nothing. The ground where the opening was had far less leaves and no twigs which made it a lot quieter to move on. Derek decided to advance slowly to stay as silent as he could. He crept past the light on the stick and towards the foot of the hill that began the long climb up Dragon's Peak.

Suddenly, there was some rustling from the tent. Neek! Derek looked to his right and then to his left and saw a large rock. As quickly as he could, he dived behind it for cover. Sure enough, out came Neek. He came out in his usual clothes, minus the cloak. He turned and reached into the tent and pulled out a massive sword. Still in the holder, it was about as long as Neek is tall. He strapped it to his back and threw his cloak on over the top. After pulling the lamp down and extinguishing it, Neek pulled the stick out from the ground and threw it to one side. He gave his neck a loud crack and stretched his hands over his head before letting out a large yawn.

Derek could hear the obvious, powerful, heavy feet of Neek, the former Zeehan Sir and hero of the land, as he began his ascent up the hill. Derek didn't move, hoping that some form of power made him both invisible and silent. Thankfully, Neek didn't seem to notice Derek and he walked on up the path ahead of him. After Neek was out of sight, he decided to follow behind him.

Derek maintained the tried and tested technique of 'low and slow' after the previous success. This time however, there wasn't much foliage to work with. The contrast between the forest and the hill was vast. While the forest was dense with green, the steepening climb was sandy and bare. Lifeless. The occasional large boulder stood out but other than that, the path was rocky and looked cut into the hill itself. There was some cover from within the pathway but no cover from anyone else that may be scaling it. Alongside the lack of cover was the fact that the higher Derek climbed, the more easily the sun could illuminate him and make him visible. The exact thing he didn't want right now.

The path continued and turned the corner, apparently spiralling around the outside of the mountain itself. He approached the corner cautiously; aware that Neek may have stopped just the other side of it. Derek couldn't hear anything, so peeped around to see that Neek was carrying on at great pace. Derek had to speed up if he wanted to keep within distance of Neek. The careful approach had to make way for a much faster one.

Derek picked himself up to something more like a jog, but still stuck close to the wall. The wall didn't really provide any cover but it definitely felt safer. Derek dashed along towards another turning that Neek had taken, this time with far less caution for being caught as he turned the corner. Around the next bend revealed a much sharper incline, almost so steep that Derek could have walked up it with his hands down. It wasn't as long and Neek had already gone out of sight over the top. The only thing Derek could do was to follow in Neek's footsteps for a bit longer.

He knew that a small hill wouldn't really slow down Neek, so Derek was quick to power up it himself. He got up quick, but his legs burned! 'Apparently I need to get better at going up hills,' he thought to himself as the sound of his own panting got louder.

At the top of the steep hill was an opening. The opening was large, big enough for at least a fifty people to set up a camp and have a party. Neek was half way across the opening by now, still under his cloak which mostly hid the huge sword strapped to his back. Derek moved behind a rock and turned in the other direction and looked out onto the land. This side of the mountain looked out to the complete opposite direction from where he lived. He couldn't see his home village or the huge main city of Zeehan either. There was some more woodland, and then some grassland and further out in the distance, Derek could just about see a huge river running right across and then bending out into the distance. Beyond that were a few more settlements, although from near they just looked like miniature figures. Beyond that still, were more mountains, far taller than the one he was on, and covered at the top with a glaze of white. Derek turned a little more to see a few clouds in the distance with, and above those clouds another mountain was towering up into heavens. It was so far and so big that he couldn't see it under the clouds, but could see it above it.

Derek gawped at the world he'd never seen until now for a little while more before regaining his focus and turning back in order to track Neek. Neek was already right over the other side and was close to entering into the next pathway, but has stopped to fiddle with the straps of his sword. Derek kept up the pursuit but did it behind the cover of the rocks as much as he could. Derek was now much closer to Neek, within only about 20 metres, and Neek stood up again and set off towards the path.

Derek watched as Neek walked up to the start of the next path when he was suddenly blown backwards. It almost looked like a lightning bolt struck Neek, a loud crack and band filled the air and Neek's cloaked body was thrown backwards. There was a huge burst of light as well and sparks flew through the air. Neek's body landed with a dusty thud on the sandy ground.

"Well, well, well... I thought I might see you here you rusty old git." Karakwat, the Dragoon, came out from behind a group of rocks on the other side of the opening. "I didn't think I'd get a chance to kick your arse again so soon, Neek."

XXXI

Neek, oddly calm after being blown off of his feet, stood up and brushed himself off. "Wondered when you'd show up. Did you not meet my friend Mr Kelderan? He was meant to hold you up."

"Yeah he tried. Thankfully that sneaky weasel Beef already had the documents drawn up. He bragged the other day that he knew all about this former official living in that village. He's a smart guy at least."

"Can't deny that. No matter what, I certainly have to agree with you. He is a weasel." They both laughed. "So why are you working for him?"

"C'mon, Neek. I'm a mercenary. The pay was way too good. And there was also the chance to come face to face with you again."

"These are trying times. Have to take any chance to earn a bit of gold and see an old friend."

"Exactly. Well, are you going to make me wait or are you going to show me this new sword you have hidden away there."

"I thought you were here to stall me."

"Nah, didn't you see what just happened? Beef set runes here to block you days ago. You won't be able to get through until he gets here. And he's not due for a while."

"So you're just here to kill that dragon?"

"No Neek, I'm under orders to leave the dragon alone. I'm actually just here to kill you."

"A Dragoon that can't kill a dragon? That's like having a pair of shoes you can't walk in. Didn't think you'd let a little squirt like Beef clip your wings."

"Shut your rusty old mouth, Neek. I'm sorry for what happened in Pa'Sa'Yha. But now you're all washed up and it's kind of sad to see what's left of you. I think it might just be kindest to put you out of your misery and save whatever is left of your dignity."

Neek removed his cloak and unbuckled his sword. He let it fall to the ground. The tip of the sword, in its hilt, faced down and so landed in the ground first, denting it. The rest of the sword fell to the ground with a thud, picking up dust as it landed. It was clearly very heavy. Karakawt drew her long spear from behind her back, holding it in two hands and taking up a stance with the tip pointing at Neek.

"You asked about the sword. It's a Luuwafal."

"Master crafted. I'm impressed. Luuwafal does make good swords."

"It's a heavy class sword, all my usual embedded runes, you know my style."

"So it'll have *colideera*, *ethidira*, *nurayaga* and *oliyaga*… power boost, speed boost, defence boost and damage reduction. Can't teach an old dog new tricks, aye Neek."

"Exactly."

Neek unsheathed the sword. The blade glistened and gleamed bright in the sunlight. He gripped the black hilt and faced Karakawt. The blade was wide, as wide as a plank of wood, and on the flat surface of the sword were four glowing ancient characters; the magically powered runes that were now empowering Neek even more. It was a common practice for adventurers to power their swords and armours with runes, but it took a true master to craft a weapon that could utilise powerful magical boosts. Luuwafal was a well-known weapon maker. The sword was powerful enough to take on most, if not all, powerful beasts of the world, but how would it fare against an equally powerful Dragoon, wielding an equally high level spear?

The two stood absolutely still, staring at one another. Neek, in his casual clothes (simple boots, baggy trousers, tunic with a few leather forearm guards) and Karakawt, in her brilliant Dragoon armour and helmet. There was a considerable gap between the two; maybe the length of ten of Neek's swords.

Without warning, without a moment of preparation, Karakawt exploded from her spot and into the air. Her shadow swept across the ground as she moved higher and higher. As quickly as she went up she came back down, and straight towards Neek. It was clear now why they were called Dragoon's; they don't just hunt dragons, they can fly like one. The spear point faced Neek, and at just the right moment she thrust the spear straight towards Neek's neck. Neek seemed prepared for this, and lifted his sword. The spear hit the wide edge of the sword and the connection created an explosion of magical power. The epicentre of the explosion caused a crack and the surrounding area rumbled and rocked. Derek was taken off of his feet even though he was behind a rock. It was clear that Karakawt chose this vast open space for a reason.

After the initial impact, Karakawt (still in the air) bounced off the sword with a back flip and landed safely on the ground. Before she could regain her balance however, Neek was rushing in and swung a long slash at Karakawt, straight across her body, aiming to cut her straight in half. Before he could connect with her body, she moved the pole of her spear in the way and blocked it. Neek followed through with the slash and knocked her flying through the air. This time, she didn't spin and landed on her feet. Again, Neek persisted and slashed wildly and violently, sometimes with one hand and sometimes with both hands. Karakawt, like a ballet dancer, moved gracefully between the swings with the occasional parry, causing small explosions of magical energy and sparks.

Derek watched on in amazement, the power from both of them rippled through the air. He recovered his own concentration and moved on towards the pathway. Derek moved along behind multiple rocks, checking carefully before advancing. He came out from behind the next rock and made for the next, before he could get there and blast off, magical power charged from the fight and split the rock in two down the middle. Derek dived back under cover wondering if the blast was meant for him, but it seemed to just be a rouge magic attack that missed its intended mark. The rock smouldered and Derek pressed on, heart beating loudly and breath panting heavily. It wasn't safe to be here right now.

Derek pressed on closer and closer to the pathway. He came out again from behind the rock to move to the next, when he turned to see a bright light careering towards him. A magical blast of energy was firing towards him at a blistering pace. Derek froze in place, shocked and unable to move. Another split second and he'd have been struck by it, but something grabbed him at the last moment and launched him to safety. Derek remained on the ground and caught his breath. There were two arms wrapped around him still, they loosened and Derek finally turned to see the familiar face of his best friend Pippie.

XXXII

Derek stared at Pippie. Pippie stared back at Derek. They both sat motionless and still. Eventually the clattering and crashing of the two duelling warriors came back into focus and the risk of being caught up in it all was once again on Derek's mind. Pippie signalled to the path, Derek nodded and the two of them proceeded up the path and away from the epic battle. They turned a corner and out of sight of Neek and Karakawt. Derek stopped and turned to face Pippie.

"Pip… what are you doing here?"

"Saving your life, apparently."

"Yeah, thanks. How did you know I was here?"

"How did I know you would come up Dragon's Peak after you said you wanted to save the dragon?"

"Fair point. Anyway, thanks for coming Pip."

"I'm sorry for what I said. You were right Derek; this is our adventure."

"It's our first adventure."

"Our first and possibly our last if we aren't careful."

"Nearly was! Oh hey, how come the invisible wall didn't get us? Neek got zapped earlier."

"It's a type of entrapment magic. Remember Neek said that Beef was good with runes? Must have been his doing. He set a trap to keep Neek from the top and must have hired that Dragoon to keep Neek occupied."

"Where is Beef?"

"He's been mobilising all of his troops this morning. They're moving as a group; there's about twenty of them, so they're moving kind of slow. I was able to set off before them and outrun them here. But they're probably not too far away now we don't have a lot of time, Derek."

"Right, let's get moving."

The two boys set off double pace. Pippie had gotten there before Beef and his men and Neek was now behind them. There was nothing between them and the top of Dragon's Peak.

They continued to climb the winding path through the mountain. The incline was steep and tough to continue up but they kept moving. The two boys turned another corner to find a narrow walkway with an old sign, made of wood, leaning up against the rock. The sign had a crudely drawn figure of a man with a large red 'X' across it. After which another crudely drawn depiction of a lizard or dragon and only the bottom half of a man hanging out of said lizard or dragon head. "This must be the place," said Pippie, with a smirk. Derek continued to lead them up the tight pathway.

The tight path turned sharply to the right and opened up more, it was beginning to feel like they were never going to reach the top. The new path was still narrow, but this time it hugged the side of the mountain and showed the very severe drop all the way back down to the bottom if even a single foot was put wrong. Derek and Pippie had to slow down, they pressed up against the rock of the mountain and side stepped across. Sliding the front foot forward and the back foot to meet it. Right, left, right, left, slowly and safely. Small pieces of broken stone crumbled under their feet and took the huge decent. They were so high now that they couldn't see the rock reach the very bottom. Birds flew under them in the distance, popping in and out from nests they'd made in the side of the mountain or up from the forest that spread across the backdrop.

The mountain this high was taller and much thinner, and the boys carefully traversed around half of it. Finally, the path gave in to a safer place to stand and the boys stopped at the new opened up area. Derek let out a huge sigh of relief and looked out into the distance of this world that he had only just discovered since climbing this mountain.

"It's amazing, aye Pip?"

"…"

"Pip? You all right?" Derek turned to see Pippie white as a sheep, face long and frozen in place. "Pip mate, what's up?" Finally, Derek turned to see what he was looking at. The peak of Dragon's Peak. It was like a cave, except the opening was big enough to fit a four-story building. It was easily as wide as it was tall, like a huge gaping mouth open at the top of the mountain. It was difficult to see inside, however, because the sun was at an odd angle, casting a ghostly shadow over the threshold.

"I hope this dragon didn't have a problem fitting into that hole, Derek. If it's hungry we might make a nice little nibble."

The two young adventurers began to walk, passing through the light and heat of the sun, into the damp darkness of the cave.

XXXIII

The cave at the top of Dragon's Peak was damp. The rock somehow slightly wet with the occasional droplets of water echoing as they splat on the ground. All the sounds that were made within it; water, the scurrying of insects, the walking of two young adventurers, all seemed to be amplified and echoed within the walls. The eyes took a few moments to adjust, and when they did, looking back outside was impossible. It was just gold light with no details.

Derek looked around and took in his new surroundings. The floor was slightly slippery in here as well, making it harder to move. Derek lowered his voice to a whisper:

"Can you see anything?"

"Only rocks. You?"

"Same."

"Do you think we were wrong?"

"Wrong about what?"

"You know, the dragon, Derek."

"I dunno. There's nothing really much here by the looks of it."

A loud, deep, bloodcurdling sound bellowed through the cave. Derek felt his spine seize up and his arms go rigid. He looked at Pippie who was wide eyed and looking back at him.

This time, a loud snorting sound filled the cave. Derek looked around frantically to find the source. Somehow, through the almost crippling fear, Derek persisted deeper. He felt Pippie's hand on his shoulder, and they continued together. Another sound, this time the scraping of something dry across the rocky ground. Deeper they went. Another snort. And then a deep breath. And again the sound of something dragging on the ground.

The grip on Derek's shoulder suddenly tightened up painfully. He swung around to see Pippie frozen in terror looking back over Derek's shoulder the other way, eyes fixated. Derek turned slowly to finally find the source of all the noises.

In the shadows, and hard to see unless you really looked, was a hulking great lump of moving 'something' sat up against the cave wall. It was long, as long as maybe twenty horses, and as tall almost as the cave itself. It was fat and round, like a giant blob. But the more Derek looked, the more he could make out; huge arms with scaly fingers each with incredible talons protruding to a needle sharp tip. A leg as wide as Derek's entire house and then some, also with toes holding the biggest talons that must have ever existed. Big enough to pierce the mountain itself. Finally Derek noticed the long tail that was probably a lot more visible than anything else. As if hidden in sight. He could see that the tail was covered in strict lines of scales that folded all in the same direction without a single fault.

Another loud snorting noise and Derek looked to the top of the shadowy blob to see the opening of an eyelid. The eye was as big as Neek's whole body, yellow, with a strip of black in the middle. A voice unlike any he'd ever heard before, deep and authoritative, echoed through the cave:

"Who goes there?"

Pippie remained silent. Derek didn't know what to say.

"WHO GOES THERE?" This time the voice bellowed. "I won't ask you again!"

"I… erm… I do." Derek finally spoke up.

"Who are you?"

"D… D… Derek."

"WHAT?"

"DEREK! My name is Derek."

"Hmm… Derek… you must speak louder, you little creature, my hearing isn't as good as it once was."

"Oh… erm… I'm sorry."

"What brings you here? Derek?"

"Well… I… erm… well, y'see, I heard there was a dragon up here and…"

"You came looking for a dragon, eh? Well, did you find one?"

"Erm… well… I thought you might be?"

"Me? You took a look at me and thought I was a dragon? What gave it away? The tail? My pointy fingers? My face?" At that moment, the massive figure moved. The head of the dragon, long and lizard-like with nostrils big enough to hide a horse in, a huge mouth with teeth taller than any man, came forward and into sight for Derek. The head turned so that the huge eye could face him, and overshadow him.

"So you are a dragon?"

"HAHAHAHHAA," the cave walls rumbled, "yes I am a dragon, what else would I be? Silly little boy, of course I'm a dragon."

"…"

"What do you want? Why have you come here?"

"Well… erm… we think someone is coming to kill you!"

"Me? Kill me? HAHAHAHHAA," the walls rumbled again, "who would dare challenge me?"

"Well you see, there's a guy that wants to come and slay you, and there's this other guy that we think might want to capture you."

"Capture now? These people must be incredibly brave or incredibly stupid."

"Someone once told me there isn't any difference."

"Very wise! Yes, I see you're much smarter than you appear little Derek. And what about this mute creature with you?"

"I… I… I'm Pip." Pippie finally squeezed out his own name.

"Pip… hmmm… stupid name."

"Well what's your name, dragon?" Derek spoke up once again.

"My name does not translate well into your silly modern language; you people are too stupid for the complexities of it. My name, as I speak it, is

Icdaranfactulalalaficgurtafluezicangokuku."

"Ic… erm…"

"HA! You see? You little creatures cannot comprehend my name."

"Well what do humans call you?"

"Enemy."

There was a chilling silence. Derek and Pip looked at each other, terrified. The dragon could well be playing with them before making them its food. They looked back at the dragon;

there isn't much escape now if that's the case. The dragon spoke again.

"You humans can be evil creatures. Most of you would try and slay a dragon like me at a moment's notice."

"That sucks, I think dragons are cool."

"Of course you do, little creature, but you'll change your mind when you get older."

"Sorry to butt in but we don't have much time." Pippie seemed to have found his voice. "Beef will be on his way soon, either that or Neek could get up here, or Karakawt."

"Karakawt? That brat is here?"

"Look, erm… Mr Dragon?"

"Yes, Mister."

"Mister Dragon, people have found out you were here and either want to come and kill you or capture you. We were ahead of them but I don't know how long for. You need to get out of here."

The dragon moved slightly again, which meant that to Derek and Pippie's perspective he moved around the cave quite a long way. Now, out of the darkness, they could see him properly. He was indeed, very fat. He also had two large wings, only they were torn and broken. The dragon breathed heavily from the movement, and then coughed and spluttered away from the young boys. The cough let out huge torrents of hot air and soot. The dragon turned to the boys again:

"I am unable to fly; I am on my last legs."

"Wait, so Neek probably could kill you right now?" Derek asked.

"Most warriors would make short work of me. This isn't ideal, I didn't plan on dying just yet."

"What can we do to help?"

"Can you fight off a high level Dragoon and whatever else is coming?"

"No."

"Then I suppose there isn't much."

"Sorry, I'm just a Turnip Knight in training."

"A what?"

"A Turnip Knight, I want to be a Turnip Knight." There was a long pause.

"HAHAHAHAHHAHHA!" The cave rumbled again; the dragon then coughed hard. "You silly humans with your translations… a Turnip Knight? That's the most ridiculous one yet."

"Yes, I know there's no such thing as a Turnip Knight I just…"

"You're wrong."

XXXIV

"When I say you're wrong, I mean you've got it wrong. It's not a 'Turnip Knight, you just got the word wrong."

"But there is a kind-of Turnip Knight?"

"You need to stop saying 'Turnip Knight', it's stupid. You sound stupid, stop sounding stupid."

"Tell me then!"

"Silence!" There was a short pause. "The name is from another language, a different language again from my name, the language of the ancient people of *Siogodden.* Are you familiar with the ancient people of *Siogodden?* No? Okay well then be quiet."

"Hundreds of years ago, in an ancient land, there was a small village, a tribe. They were warriors primarily, as defending their village was paramount. At some point, however, they began to dabble in the art of taming familiars. It isn't uncommon to have an animal with you, but they took it a step further and tried their luck with bigger beasts. Like dragons."

"Long story short is that they were completely unsuccessful, and eventually the fascination with taming a dragon wiped them out. However, some braniac decided that rather than trying to tame a dragon, it would be smarter to work with it. Many powerful forces were making moves across different parts of the world in the pursuit of domination and power, and it was causing the death of many people and the mass extinction of many more creatures. So, we decided to work with these people."

"We?"

"Yes, we. Stop interrupting. We worked together, me and other dragons with a few humans, and we studied some pretty serious magic and developed something entirely new. We created a type of bonding mechanism whereby we, the dragons, could create a bond with a human. Turns out, it also worked on elves as well but I haven't seen it work with others, probably does with dwarves."

"Wait, so you worked with humans and elves and stuff for hundreds of years?"

"Yes, little Derek creature. And there was a name given to this contracted bond. *Tŭrnip Knáárt.* Which I would assume has somehow translated to 'Turnip Knight' along the way."

"What does it mean?"

"It means 'the bonding of two species for the good of all' or something like that."

"Pip… the story is true!"

"Not true, I just told you the translation was wrong."

"I can actually become a Turnip Knight."

"No you can't, I literally just explained to you that you were wrong. And also you can't because not anyone can complete the bond. Only those with pure soul and an innate power are able to withstand the transition into the bond of *Tŭrnip Knáárt.* After the host human dies, the bond is re-sealed into a talisman and can only be worn by those that are chosen based on the conditions I just mentioned. If you are not worthy then the talisman is a useless lump of metal. If you are worthy then you can begin the Pilgrimage to Power and complete assimilation to the dragon."

Now that the dragon had moved, Derek could see a large wooden chest in the corner. It had no padlock, and looked extremely old.

"You've spotted my chest, I see. Within the chest holds the talisman, if it was meant for one of you runts then it would glow bright. As you'll see now it is not going to glow bright as it isn't for you."

The dragon's massive hands reached out and picked up the chest as if it weighed nothing. He held it in the palm of one hand and placed one of his massive scaly fingers on one side and another on the other. He presented the chest to Derek and opened it. The moment it opened, there was a brilliant bright light that shone out from it. The dragon didn't quite notice at first, but finally he looked and saw that the chest was gleaming.

"WHAT? YOUUUUU!"

Derek and Pippie looked at each other. The dragon dropped the chest to the ground in disbelief and the talisman, shining bright like a small sun, fell out. Derek picked it up. It wasn't too heavy and it fit in the palm of his hand perfectly. Attached was a simple red string. The talisman continued to glow but got less bright, and it began to shake and vibrate in his hand.

Derek looked up at the dragon, which seemed to have as much a surprised look as a dragon could make with its face, and he pulled the two ends of string apart and put it over his head.

The talisman now hung around Derek's neck.

There was a shake and a vibration from the talisman and the brightness came again. The dragon began moving strangely as well, contorting and twisting. The talisman got brighter and brighter and it was too bright not to cover the eyes.

As quickly as it got bright, the brightness completely went away. Derek and Pippie unshielded their eyes and looked around to find the cave empty. The huge dragon seemed to have gone. A tiny, slightly squeaky voice came from above. "Well that's just my luck… dammit."

They looked up to see a new dragon, this one was tiny. The size of Derek or maybe even a bit smaller. It was red with scales and had a short stumpy face with big eyes. Sticking out behind it were little wings and it had a stumpy but much more slender body than the last dragon. The dragon came down slowly and landed with its stumpy legs on the ground. It became clear to the two boys that this was in fact the same dragon.

"So what's happened here is that my body will change to match the person I'm paired to. The last guy I was partnered with ended up super fat in the end. So now I'm a little runt like you! Dammit I hope I don't see anyone I know; they'll be teasing me for this one!"

"Wait… so I'm a Turnip Knight now?"

"No! You're just connected with me! You aren't a *Tŭrnip Knáárt* yet, you're just some brat with a dragon."

"Cool!"

"Yeah maybe for you but now I'm stuck with you for however long you runts live for."

"Yes! I'm going to become super strong now and we'll travel around the world together!"

"Maybe save getting out the party hats for a minute here, Derek. It looks like things weren't quite that smooth. I'm not connected to you."

"What? But I'm wearing the talisman, it was shining and everything!"

"Yeah, I'm connected to you but I'm also connected to Mr Mute over here." Pippie looked confused. "Yeah, you. Looks like we're a triple threat! Never seen this before, must be something to do with you two."

"Derek," Pippie broke his silence, "you remember the spell? We must have some kind of connection! Neek did say he'd never seen anyone cast that spell on someone else like I did!"

"Both of you look at your shoulder." They both did, and saw an emblem of a lizard with its mouth open similar to the one painted on the sign on the way up, but without the half eaten person on it. "Yeah, see, you both got my insignia on you. Looks like we're all one big team now. I can feel the energy of a warrior mainly in you, Derek, but Pip you're surging with powerful magic energy. This might actually work really well. Listen, I can't really fight these guys and I'm worn out from changing forms and all that... so I'm gonna' just disappear into that talisman for a bit."

The dragon turned into a kind of cloud and the cloud was eaten up into the talisman around Derek's neck. The boys looked at each other and back at their dragon insignias on their arms. "My mum's gonna' kill me."

XXXV

Derek and Pippie let the bright light of the sun bake their faces once again. Their eyes adjusted and the dark cave they'd come from dulled out of vision. Derek lifted his hand to cover his eyes during the transition. In the light, however, there was a different kind of darkness. The familiar sight of green markings and the snobby, arrogant slim face of Sir Beef Stroganoff and a group of roughly twenty of his men stood before Derek and Pippie.

"You two little maggots… In the name of the Zeehan Kingdom I demand you answer; state your business up here."

"Nothing, sir," chimed Pippie, "my friend Derek and I are just minding our own business."

"Hmm… seize them!"

Four men came out from the side of the crowd and quickly grabbed the two boys, holding them tightly. Without another word and ignoring the cries and struggles from Derek and Pippie, Sir Beef walked slowly and smoothly straight through and into the cave. With a small wave of his arm the cave lit up with a spell. Every nook and cranny of the cave was revealed as clear as day. The boys hadn't noticed when the cave was under the cover of shade that walls had deep claw marks. They could have been old or they could have been recent, some claw marks were cut inches and even feet deep into the stone. Whatever had done it had cut into the rock like knife through butter. There was a set of claw marks in particular that spanned the entire height of the cave, and at their deepest could fit Derek or Pippie inside of it.

Sir Beef's men searched the cave. The only thing they could find was the chest that previously had the talisman inside it that Derek how had around his neck. Quickly, quietly and carefully, Derek slipped the talisman under his shirt while maintaining his eye contact firmly on Sir Beef.

Three of the guards lifted the chest and moved it closer to Sir Beef for inspection. He ruffled in the chest and found nothing. Sir Beef swore quietly under his breath and kicked the chest, visibly hurting his foot. He turned and limped towards the two boys, grabbed Pippie by his shirt and pulled him in.

"You. You two little fools. Where is my dragon?"

"Ouch! Get off me!"

"Tell me where my dragon is!"

"Oooooouch!" Sir Beef threw Pippie to the ground.

"Where has that blasted Dragoon gone?"

Karakawt, the Dragoon, walked into the cave. Her armour was beaten and half hanging off. Her left eye was completely shut from a bruise, like she'd been punched incredibly hard in the face. The right side of her helmet was broken off and all both wings that she previously had were gone. One of her arms was bleeding and she looked like she'd been dragged multiple times through the sandy mud.

"Here. What do you want?"

"I want my dragon!"

"Well I'm a Dragoon, not a dragon. Stupid runt." Karakawt span a thick wad of blood on the ground.

"What was that? I was assured there would be a dragon up here. You're the dragon expert and I'm paying you more than enough, tell me what happened."

Karakawt walked deeper into the cave and looked around. She examined the claws and the chest carefully. She then looked up and sniffed. She sniffed in many directions and then finally started sniffing towards Derek. Karakawt's expression changed from stern to even more stern. She glared at Derek for a moment and turned back to Sir Beef.

"Looks like it's gone."

"WHAT?"

"There's definitely traces, it's been here recently and it left that chest. But it's gone now. Sorry."

"Gone where? Surely we'd have seen it fly away. It's not a bird!"

"Look, it was here, and now it isn't. That's it. I've done my job, I kept Neek busy, and I'd like my pay now."

"Your pay? Ugh, fine, give her the money." One of Sir Beef's men handed Karakawt a jingling bag of coins.

"This bag is a little light. You undercutting me, Beef?"

"That's *Sir* Beef to you, Dragoon. You got what is fair considering there is no dragon. Now get lost."

"No way! That wasn't the deal, Beef."

"You dare to talk down to a Zeehan Sir? Get out of my face now or I'll have you blacklisted as a mercenary."

"Fine… cya."

Karakawt turned and walked out of the cave. One of the men holding Derek spoke up:

"Sir, what do we do with these two?"

"We have no need for them; just throw them off of there. Don't worry they're young they'll just bounce off the ground!"

Derek and Pippie looked at each other with their eyes open and started struggling again. The men started dragging the boys out of the cave. Derek and Pippie yelled and screamed, kicking and biting at the men holding them down. Derek felt a swift punch in the gut that took the wind out of him and he feel limp for a moment from the pain.

Pippie tried to go limp in the body and drag his heels in the ground to slow himself down. He twisted and turned, trying to elbow his holders. The boys got closer and closer to the edge of the mountain. The trees were small below, it was almost impossible to see individual trees without squinting the eyes. As they got over the edge, Derek felt a sinking feeling through his chest and down into the bottom of his feet. He began to breath loudly and struggle again, begging the men not to throw them over the edge. His chest tightened and took his breath away. His feet and hands tingled and an almighty ache came over his body. The fear of falling to his death took over.

The grip on Derek and Pippie's arms loosened and they were let go.

XXXVI

Derek and Pippie fell, but they weren't quite over the edge and managed to keep from falling off. Derek turned to see the men that were holding them were completely gone. He turned more to find them on the ground a few metres away. On the other side of them was the shadow of a very beaten up man. Burten Neek stood above them. No cloak, but extremely bruised and beaten. The entire right side of his body was red with blood and what was left of his trousers barely covered his legs at all. Neek's face was patchy with bruises and sandy mud. He looked down at the two boys.

"You two shouldn't be here, it's not safe."

"I thought I put you down enough, Neek." Karakawt said with a small snigger.

"You did me pretty good, but I managed to get up. Were you really going to let these two get thrown off the edge?"

"Nah, I was just waiting a little longer before stepping in. May as well make it a bit more dramatic."

"You been paid?"

"I was short-handed. That stuck up toad over there didn't give me what he promised."

Sir Beef barged his way through his crowd of men.

"Karakawt, finish him off!"

"No."

"You will do as you are asked!"

"I've been paid! I don't work for you anymore you horrible little weasel. Neek is kind of a friend, so I'm not going to harm another hair on his head for nothing."

"I'll pay you! Just deal with him."

"No."

"What?"

"You haven't even paid me enough for the job I was actually contracted to do! So I think I'll politely decline, thanks."

"Why you arrogant... Men, these two are weakened from their battle together. Take them out!"

There was a hesitation from the men... and then they began to advance. Arrows flew into the air and swordsmen drew their swords and charged, yelling.

"Boys, you need to leave, now." Neek said, drawing his sword. "Get down this mountain as quickly as you can."

Without another word, Derek and Pippie darted for the narrow path leading off the mountain. Behind them, they could hear the yelling of warriors battling. Arrows pinging off metal and the sparking of spells hitting their mark. They didn't look back; they just continued to flee as quickly as they could.

They got out from the narrow path and continued down. Still silent, they ran as fast as they could downhill. Moving downhill was much easier than up. They quickly reached the large opening where Neek and Karakawt fought. The ground was still smouldering from the massive battle, and there were many marks on the ground where spells and wayward sword and spear attacks had cut into the ground. They continued to run and run, down Dragon's Peak's mountain and back towards the forest. Finally, they turned the corner and found themselves back at ground level where Derek first saw Neek set off this morning. The boys stopped for the first time, suddenly realising how tired they were from the running. They panted heavily from the run and let their hearts slow down. Derek wiped the sweat from his forehead.

"You think… you think it was right to run?"

"Y… y… yes… I'm out of shape…"

"What now?"

"I don't know. Back to the village?"

The boys started for the forest and back to the village. Feeling like danger was now much further away they slowed themselves to a walk. Derek noticed that the path was more trodden now than when he came through here before. It must have been from Sir Beef's men. Paths that have a lot of traffic naturally end up more trodden in, and usually no one comes this far out for fear of meeting a monster or a dragon.

"What about this medal thing, Pip?"

"It's a talisman, not a medallion?"

"Well I feel like we kind of won it, so it's kind of a medallion."

"No, that's a medal."

"Exactly."

"What? Anyway, I think we just need to hold onto it for a bit. I don't know what we can trust now."

"Well Beef tried to give us the fast route to the bottom, Neek wanted to kill our new friend inside it, and the Dragoon is specialised in killing dragons."

"What about Kelderan?"

"He was in on it with Neek; he'd want to kill it, too."

"Oh yeah. Maybe we can ask my dad?"

"Isn't he a news guy?"

"A reporter. He may have an idea what to do."

"You think he'd like your new tattoo?"

"I forgot about that! Your mum is gonna' dent her ladle on your head, Derek!"

"Yeah well don't think she'll hold back on you either!"

The boys made it back to the route that Derek knew. At the turning to the safe rope bridge and the practice tree. At this time of day there wasn't much threat in that area from monsters attacking, so they continued on without much fear. They made it back to the road to find the makeshift camp setup by Sir Beef, many of his men were still there but they seemed to be in some kind of panic.

The boys proceeded towards the village with caution, going around the most obvious route straight through the middle of the camp. When they got to the other side, they noticed four men dressed slightly differently. They were all in armour similar to the armoured men that Sir Beef had, but they had blue markings on their armour rather than green. Three of the men were dressed the same, one was roughly half a foot taller and had on his back a much larger sword with multiple spikes sticking out all the way up the blade. He didn't wear a helmet and instead had long, straight black hair. He was talking to a few of Sir Beef's men who looked visibly scared.

The boys got further around and got to see the man's face; he was pale but had no blemishes on his face at all. His eyes were dazzling blue and he held his head high. He turned to see Derek and Pippie as they tried to slyly pass through the commotion and back into the village. A commanding voice called out: "You two! Come here!" Derek turned to see it was him calling them over.

XXXVII

"Sir Elhan, these kids are just a couple of trouble makers."

"These trouble makers have just come from the forest in the direction of the mountain and are covered in dry dust, which is exactly the terrain of said mountain. Now go annoy someone else." The guard with green markers walked away.

"You two. You heard my name, now tell me yours."

"I'm Derek and this is Pip."

"Derek and Pip. Strange names. Where is Sir Beef?"

"We don't know who that is."

"If you're going to play dumb then at least make it believable. I know you know who he is."

"He knows I know who he knows… what?"

"You aren't too bright are you? What about you, Pip? Are you the brains here?"

"I know who Sir Beef is. Why should I tell you anything?" Pippie tried to sound authoritative in his tone of voice.

"I'm just here trying to clean up this mess. Putting a village on lockdown, imprisoning an old man, permitting a lot of money to hire some mercenary… sometimes we Zeehan Sirs have to monitor each other. Now will you tell me what you know?"

The boys looked at each other and nodded. Pip obliged.

"He was up the top of Dragon's Peak. Karakawt, the Dragoon, was hired to fight with Neek so he could go after the dragon."

"Neek is there? Just as I suspected. And the dragon?"

"Well there weren't any. We got there first and there was no dragon, just an empty chest. So Beef tried to have us thrown off the top but Neek and Karakawt stepped in and saved us."

"He tried to have you thrown off the top?" Elhan sighed. "I'm sorry to hear that happened. I will be sure to have a word with him. You should probably run along home now, I'll handle it from here."

"And what are you going to do?" Derek spoke up again.

"I don't think that's any of your business."

"Well one of you Sirs tried to kill us. Also, that Beef had us locked in our village and his bully guards have been pushing us around now for ages!"

"I see you've lost a lot of trust in us because of him. Very well. When he gets back down he will have to pack up this camp before coming back to the castle, so I'll be waiting here for him. I'm also writing up a report so that I can give that directly to the king himself. His actions may have rendered him a liability and he may lose his place. Does that satisfy you?"

"You should punch him in the face as well."

"I prefer to deal with situations legally and without violence, but I'll certainly consider it. Now off you two go. Can I rely on you for interview if I need it further down the line?"

"Yeah, you can count on me and Pip. Anything to get back at Beef."

"Careful how you speak, he is still a Zeehan Sir and his men here are loyal to him. Speak no more ill words about him and go home, both of you. And I recommend you wash and change your clothes, you're both sweaty and dirty."

The boys made their way back into the village. It felt like a short lifetime since Derek had seen the usual mud huts and wooden buildings that made up his beloved home. People were out more than usual and there was no sign of any of Beef's men. The men were preparing tools again to restart their work that they'd been forced to stop during the lockdown. Deegal Dimmie was out, chatting with everyone and cracking jokes. Derek felt a small feeling of accomplishment, like he'd been directly involved in saving the village from evil. It felt good.

Derek and Pippie parted ways to head back to their own homes. It wasn't long before Derek got back home to find his mother waiting for him outside. He was surprised to find that a hug awaited him rather than a ladle whack around the head. He was also greeted to a tasty stew. But not before washing; Derek's mother noticed that he was dirty just like Elhan said.

As quickly as things escalated, they seemed to calm down. Derek was back to being at home with his mother and eating stew. Only now he had a talisman with a dragon emblem and a dragon insignia on his arm. Derek didn't speak to Mr Kelderan about what happened but he was freed from the imprisonment of Sir Beef's men. Derek couldn't know for sure but it doesn't look like his plan worked all that well.

XXXVIII

The next day, the lockdown was officially lifted and everything was starting to return to normal. Derek and Pip met up and went out to the practice tree together. The camp was gone by the next day and the only signs that they were ever there were the marks in the ground where the tent pegs had been knocked into the mud. They made it to the practice tree when the high pitched voice of the dragon spoke out for the first time:

"Well. This has all been a bit of a crazy experience!"

"Wooow! Wait you can talk from there?" Derek was astonished.

"Yeah I can talk. Sorry I didn't before, I needed to lay low and rest. That brat Karakawt can be a pain in the arse when she wants to be. Glad you weren't thrown off the edge, though. I would've had to step up."

"You could have saved us?"

"I think so. I mean, probably."

"You only think so?"

"My body isn't quite what it used to be, kid. Usually catching two runts like you wouldn't be a problem, but these aren't usual times. It doesn't matter now anyway. You got out of it and you're still alive so that's good I suppose. You two have a lot of work to do now you've taken on this contract with me."

"Oh yeah. I thought we'd be super powerful now but I don't feel any different. Do you know how to use magic now Pip?"

"Nope."

"Idiots... you don't just... get bestowed with near limitless strength. What good would you be? I could find you the strongest sword ever forged but you wouldn't know *how* to swing it. Did you forget our first conversation? I told you that you needed to go on the Pilgrimage of Power."

"And where is that?"

"Well actually you're in luck. It isn't that far from here. It's about a hundred miles south."

"A HUNDRED! Wait is that far?"

"Compared to how big this world is, no. The Zeehan Kingdom is about four miles from here in the other direction."

"I've never been further away than the city; that seems really far away."

"It's all relative, Derek."

"I don't have any family down south I don't think."

"No, I meant... oh it doesn't matter. I'm coming out."

The mist that pushed its way into the talisman the day before started to leak out. The mist got bigger and thicker and eventually the familiar sight of the now small red dragon materialised in front of them, hovering with its small wings fluttering to keep it afloat. It stretched and yawned and turned and twisted as if it'd been stuck in a small box.

"Right then. If you want to become *Týrnip Knáárt* you'll have to travel and complete the Pilgrimage of Power."

"How should we tell our mums, Pip?"

"Don't know, how should I pack?"

"Listen you two. That stuff isn't important. You both hold within you the potential to become legends in your own right. Only you can step up to the challenge."

From out of the dense forest, came a familiar, rusty voice. "I knew you two were up to something. Well done, boys." Neek appeared.

XXXIX

Neek was clean of blood, but still very much bruised. His face had a few marks although a lot was covered by his beard. He had his cloak on again but with the hood down.

"Derek, I told you not to go up there."

"Yeah well Derek decided he had his own plan." The dragon spoke up for the boys.

"A talking creature? I've never seen anything like this before."

"Hey, don't you go talking at me like I'm some worthless object. You got your butt handed to you on a plate up the mountain the other day and you don't want to make matters worse for yourself."

"How did you know about all that?"

"Duh, I'm the dragon you were looking for you knuckle head."

"You? Boys, get back, that thing is dangerous." Neek very quickly drew his sword and stood prepared to attack, but Derek tried to reason with him.

"No! It's fine, he's with us."

"I don't trust monsters, Derek, and you shouldn't either."

At that moment Neek lunged forward at speed and thrust his sword straight at the dragon. The boys gasped but weren't fast enough to do anything. The dragon, however, moved gracefully. He jumped over the lunging thrust and twisted into a spin. He whirled himself around and smashed Neek hard in the head with his tail. Neek face planted the ground, making a small dent in the forest floor. The dragon landed on the ground just as gracefully as he had launched himself into the air.

"Look here you sword swinging lunatic, I'm no threat to anyone here. That is anyone here but you if you come at me with that sword again. Now calm yourself down before I do you worse than I did in Daburan."

"Daburan? What? How is that possible…"

Neek finally calmed down and but his sword away and sat peacefully with the two boys and the dragon. The dragon explained how the connection worked between warrior and beast and how Derek and Pippie were the new joint warriors that he was connected to. He also went on to explain that he was much larger and fatter because the old warrior was, but now he was dead.

"Wait, so the man I was tracking before has died?"
"Afraid so, he conked in back in Daburan so I had to return here."

"How did he die? When we fought he was so powerful."
"He choked."
"Choked?"
"Yeah, on a carrot."
"He choked on a carrot?"
"Yeah. Tragic, really."

"The strongest warrior I've ever come across in my entire life that so easily bested me in battle… died from choking on a carrot?"

"That's what I said. He did love his carrots."

"I don't know what to say."

"Oh it's okay I don't need your condolences."

"I didn't mean…"

"At least he died doing what he loved; eating a carrot."

"…"

The dragon went back into the talisman and the boys, now accompanied by Neek, walked back to Doko Village. Neek knew that Kelderan lived next to Derek and wanted to see him. Pippie decided to go along with them as he wasn't due home for another few hours.

They walked together through Doko Village, drawing a bit of attention from the locals. Even without his armour and with the bruises on his face Neek was still something of a celebrity. And that celebrity walking around with two of the local kids was very strange. They walked together all the way back to Derek's house. When they finally got there they found Kelderan outside his house and surprised to see Neek. The all sat with Kelderan and he explained everything that happened. This took a while, because Kelderan constantly interrupted with his theories and pacing up and down ranting about history books and legal cases that didn't really relate to the situation. Then the conversation switched to Sir Beef, the boys stayed quiet as they tried to keep up with that was happening:

"After seeing Beef up at the top of the mountain I'm convinced that fears are true."

"You think he's been tainted?"

"Yes, I could feel his negative energy."

"Hmm… this is worrying indeed. Unprecedented, in fact." Kelderan started to pace again. "We've never had anyone tainted and not isolated from The Table of Representatives before…"

"Erm, Neek, what's it mean to be tainted?" Pippie asked Neek while Kelderan continued to rant.

"It's a dark energy. Kind of like a disease but it's intentionally inflicted. It's possible that someone at the castle has tainted Beef, or it's possible Beef wanted more power and chose it for himself. I don't know yet how bad it is or if anyone else is affected. It can make you behave maliciously, but you two already found that out when he ordered you be thrown off the mountain top."

Kelderan returned to the conversation. "What? Thrown off the mountain? Damn fool. Well this will take some monitoring and will be difficult to deal with. We can't really enlist people from another country or it might look like an invasion or power move. We need to get in and see if the King is affected."

"Agreed. I guess that's our next mission. Although with a bit of luck we'll have a couple of young, dragon wielding warriors on our side soon."

Derek's mother came out to call Derek in, but was surprised to see Neek.

"Oh my… Sir Neek!"

"Not a Sir anymore, ma'am. But yes, I have gotten to know your son here. He's quite brave."

"Brave? Well… he does take after his father; always out adventuring."

"I see. Well Derek? I think you best go and eat! You'll need your strength; you have quite the adventure coming." Neek gave Derek a little wink.

Derek and Pippie agreed to meet up again tomorrow. They had a lot to work out with the Pilgrimage of Power and how to go about it, although their new dragon friend said he would guide them the whole way. But he was very clear that no one else was allowed to help them; "this is a journey for the warrior and dragon, and only the warrior and dragon."

The sun set over Doko Village. The men had worked again for the first time and were winding down and ready for bed. Derek, the young Turnip Knight in training, turned *Ty̆rnip Knáárt* in training. But now he had a companion, his best friend, Pippie.

The sun set on Doko Village to mark the end of the day and the end of their first adventure together, but this is only the beginning of the Tales of the Turnip Knight.